MY IRISH TALE

about the Magdalene Laundry

BY JOHN HODGE

Printed and bound in the United States of America
First printing • ISBN # 978-1-954463-24-0

MY IRISH TALE

about the Magdalene Laundry

BY JOHN HODGE

SCOTT PUBLISHING COMPANY
www.scottpublishingcompany.com
P.O. Box 9707 • Kalispell, MT 59904
Toll Free: 1-800-628-0212
Fax: 1-406-756-0098

This book is dedicated to my family, who have endured a lifetime of my imaginary stories and outlandish tales.

Chapter 1

In a small village not too far removed from Galway, in a little house with a neat yard with carefully pruned trees and neatly trimmed bushes, a family drama was playing out. A young woman, her father and mother were engaged in a heated discussion. The young woman had just revealed to her parents that she was with child. Her weeping mother tried to mitigate the interchange between the angry father and the hapless young girl.

"It is no matter, dear Duff," she pleaded with her husband. "The child will be our grandchild."

"Not mine," he shouted, "not mine."

"Please," she begged, "have mercy on our daughter."

"Mercy! Mercy be damned," he shouted. "She has brought shame to our family and disgraced our family name. There is no mercy in my heart for a girl who would shame herself, disgrace her family and destroy all we have gained. She shall be banished from this house and never be spoken of again while I draw a breath. Tomorrow will be her final day under this roof."

"Mamma, Mamma please help me," the hapless young girl begged.

"I cannot," her mother replied as tears ran down her face. "Your father has decided."

The seventeen-year-old girl was on her knees with her arms around her father's legs. "No Papa, no. It was only once and he said he loved me, he said we would be married."

"Then you are stupid as well," he countered.

"Please Papa, please," the young woman wailed. "Please don't send me away."

"There is no place in our family for a girl with the morals of a vulgar animal," replied her father. You are trash and like all trash must be discarded. I will not tolerate any deleterious effect on this family because of your shameful actions. We shall be disgraced and the laughingstock of the entire village," he hissed.

The wretched young girl collapsed at her father's feet knowing there would be no forgiveness in his hard heart.

Just a few months previously, Erin O'Donnell had been at a girlfriend's house in Kilkenny. Her friend Roselyn Finn had a twenty-year-old brother, Patrick. Patrick had befriended an American sailor whose ship had stopped in Galway Bay for a couple of weeks on a goodwill visit. The sailor John was a fine looking fellow with a gift of gab who was extremely popular with the ladies. An innocent and inexperienced girl was easy prey for a rogue like John. Toward Erin, John had always been the quintessential gentleman and Erin was mesmerized by this worldly fellow from America. It took only a short time before Erin was completely relaxed with John and thought she was in love. Never was there even a hint of impropriety from John, he was biding his time while grooming an inexperienced and immature young girl.

One evening after watching a romantic film at the cinema while walking home, John professed his love to Erin and asked her to marry him when she was eighteen. Erin was overjoyed and agreed to become his bride. John asked that their engagement be kept a secret as he wanted to announce it as a Christmas surprise to his family. Of course, it would mean there would be no engagement ring, but Erin was all too happy and eager to acquiesce to this request. From that point on John pressed Erin to prove her love. He became more amorous, his kisses became more passionate and his hands began to wander. Although Erin was initially uncomfortable with this new experience, she was in love and was going to be married.

One day late in the Fall, the couple went on a picnic. The weather was brisk and John had brought along a bottle of Jameson to ward off the chill. Just a couple of sips of the whisky removed any inhibitions Erin had. John took her virginity, then took her home. He had accomplished his mission and now had bragging rights amongst his mates: "She was no show horse, but good for a ride around the barn." What a fine tale he would tell his buddies back at the ship. His reputation was intact, Third Class Petty Officer John Hodge could bed any woman he wanted.

Erin on the other hand, was troubled from the onset. The experience with John was not as wonderful and romantic as she thought it would be. It was painful and John was rough. John no longer called on Erin and she could not understand why. Her confusion turned to terror when her "Auntie" didn't visit the following month. She waited and waited but it never came. Erin contacted Roselyn's brother Patrick and asked if he had talked to John. Patrick told her John was a tosser and no longer his friend. John had been seen with a barmaid who was known for her lack of morals. Erin went down to the American destroyer and asked to see John. A messenger returned saying John did not want to see her and wanted her to stop bothering him. Erin was heartbroken. There was nothing left to do but to tell her parents.

Chapter 2

Duff O'Donnell was a successful businessman and highly respected in the community. He was on the town council and one of few Protestants who was appreciated by the Catholic majority. Because of their standing in the community, the O'Donnell's could not afford the slightest hint of scandal. A daughter pregnant out of wedlock would certainly accomplish that result.

Once apprised of her condition, Duff had no other option, and Erin would be placed in the Magdalene Laundry at Cobh, in County Cork. The Magdalene Laundries existed in every major city that was home to a hospital. All of the hospital linens and uniforms were washed and ironed by inmates at the Magdalene Laundry. Young women who had in some way offended their family, the authorities or society were often confined at the Magdalene. Their offense may have been that they were merely a little slow in learning. Others had mental problems, some were petty thieves, others were promiscuous.

The laundries never seemed to have enough inmates, so everyone was welcome if the cash donation were large enough. Cobh was on the coast and sufficiently distanced so it was unlikely that anyone would learn of the circumstances of Erin's departure. The story would be that Erin had gone to live with a relative in Dublin in order to attend school.

Chapter 3

As there were no accommodations for children, or pregnant women in the Magdalene Laundries, Erin would first be sent to a Convent until such time as the child was delivered. The Convent was a teaching institution where aspiring nuns were prepared for a life of service. Although the Convent was not set up for maternity purposes, the Sisters had previously performed the role of midwife. The nuns were quite resourceful when unexpected funds were made available. The transaction was strictly cash and the amount differed according to the size of the individual's pocket. Since the money was not officially on the Convent's records, the nuns used it for their own purposes.

First and foremost, was replenishing the supply of sacramental wine. The allotment of wine was barely sufficient for the purpose for which it was intended, and certainly not sufficient for its being enjoyed for other reasons. Several of the Sisters felt the need of a glass from time to time for various ailments, real or imaginary. Why even the fathers who routinely visited the Convent expected to enjoy a glass of wine while recovering from their arduous journeys.

The Diocese provided most all of the needs of the Convent, with a few exceptions. Milk was purchased from a local farmer, and sometimes they would receive a donation, an old hen which had ceased laying eggs, or a tough old rooster. The Diocese provided the Convent with tea, flour, sugar, salt and those vegetables which would remain edible for lengthy periods in the root cellar. Turnips, potatoes, carrots, onions and cabbage and always a generous amount of oatmeal. Meat was usually sausage, bacon and occasionally some fish.

Chapter 4

The Mother Superior of the Convent was Sister Angelia. Sister Angelia was approaching her 90th birthday and could have retired long ago. Matter of fact, she had been encouraged to retire several times. This being the only life she had ever known, she could not see herself retired. She enjoyed the power and the respect due her title. The younger Sisters were terrified of Sister Angelia and the younger priests quickly learned to stay in her good favor.

Sister Angelia had an appetite and appreciation not only for spirits but for fowls, chops, lobsters and oysters. Whenever the occasion presented itself, Sister Angelia extracted the largest donation she could from the parent who placed their hapless child in her care.

When contacted by Duff O'Donnell, Sister Angelia sensed the urgency and desperation of Erin's father. With that in mind, she drove a hard bargain and received a very sizeable donation, one of the largest she had ever gained. Sister Angela already had spent the money in her mind. With a smile on her face, she was planning a feast, one that included a bottle or two of Irish whiskey for her singular use.

Erin was taken the following day by motorcar to the Convent about two hour's drive away. The journey was a nightmare for Erin. She had been used by John, deserted by her friend and disowned by her family. Everything she had ever known was no longer a part of her life. The future was uncertain and the lifestyle Erin had enjoyed was forever to be but a memory.

With the money being exchanged from one hand to the other, Duff O'Donnell turned without saying a word, walked out the door, got into his vehicle and drove off, never looking back and never to see his daughter again.

Chapter 5

The Convent was the largest building Erin had ever seen. It was built of stone and was hundreds of years old. Ivy grew up the walls and birds inhabited the ivy. There were six teaching nuns and usually three or four aspiring nuns in training. The teaching nuns were all up in years and this would most likely be their final assignment for the church. The nuns by and large were devout and believed idle chatter was unnecessary, therefore there was little conversation other than classes and prayers. Laughter was a rarity and only when there was a priest present for the nuns to impress.

Sister Angelia was a dried-up old prune who thought she was God's avenging angel. She was extremely strict with the younger nuns and at times sadistically cruel to unfortunate girls placed in her charge. Erin, frightened and sobbing, was roughly grabbed by the arm and slapped in the face.

"Now, you worthless whore, you will do as you are told and never speak unless spoken to. You will serve here among the righteous while your bastard grows inside you. After you rid your body of the devil's child, you will spend your life making penance for your evil ways by doing the Lord's work. Your bastard child will go to the orphanage where it belongs. You will pray three times a day for your soul's salvation, though I doubt if our Lord will listen to a Protestant whore. Let me tell you, I will use the rod and put stripes on your back for any infraction of our rules, do you understand?" Erin could only nod as she was sobbing so hard. "Answer me when I address you, whore." Erin was barely able to whisper, "Yes, Sister."

"Speak up, whore," said Sister Angelia as she grabbed Erin's hair and smacked her face. Erin was in shock, barely able to comprehend what was happening to her. "Take off your clothes," ordered Sister Angelia. When Erin hesitated, Sister Angelia grabbed the front of her dress and ripped it open. "Take off your clothes," she shouted. Erin complied, and stripped down to her bra and panties. "Off you fool, take them off," yelled Sister Angelia. Unable to understand what was transpiring, Erin removed her bra, and with great shame she lowered her panties. Erin stood naked in front of the nun with tears streaming down her face. Sister Angelia had produced a willow switch about a meter long. "Now," said Sister Angelia, "do you understand?"

"Please," said Erin. Before she could finish the sentence, the willow sliced across the back of her thighs. "Yes, yes," shouted Erin, "I understand."

"Now isn't that better?" said Sister Angelia with a smirk. "Yes, Sister," replied Erin. "Follow me," said Sister Angelia and she began walking back into the building. Erin followed, trying but unable to cover her nudity with her arms. They passed several others as they went. Erin did not look up but could see the bottoms of their black habit. Some made comments as they passed. Erin could not understand everything they were saying but did hear one comment. "That's the Protestant recently delivered, and with child as well, they say."

Erin was taken to a large room with several beds. In the far corner of the room, she was shown her bed, being no more than a mattress on the floor. No sheet, just a thin blanket. She was given a plain dress to wear and a pair of well-worn shoes, no under garments and no stockings. She was shown where to bathe and admonished to be clean at all times. "It's bad enough being a whore, but a dirty whore will not be tolerated. Your father paid well to be rid of you, otherwise you would be on the streets where you belong."

Chapter 6

From that day forward, each day was a duplicate of the day before. Awakened at five o'clock, prayers for one hour. Breakfast of watery porridge, one cup of tea and a piece of bread. Washing clothes, scrubbing floors and general cleaning until noon. Lunch consisted of watery soup, bread and tea. There were never seconds and Erin was always hungry. After lunch there were prayers, then back to cleaning.

Dinner was usually cabbage or turnips sometimes with a tiny rasher of bacon. On Sundays Erin received soup, with vegetables and bits of meat in it. Even so, the portions were small, not nearly sufficient for a woman carrying a child.

The nuns on the other hand dined well. Sister Angelia had spent the money on chops, fowl, fresh eggs, even oysters and plenty of wine. The nuns enjoyed tea time in mid-morning and afternoon. Tea and biscuits with marmalade, laughing and telling tales about the priests they had encountered along the way. Occasionally, one of the nuns would leave a morsel of food or a bit of biscuit on her plate and when Erin cleared away the dishes, she would relish the crumbs left behind.

The ensuing seven and a half months dragged on. Erin was kept busy scrubbing floors and waiting on the nuns. It seemed they all hated her and went out of their way to be unkind to Erin. Even the young nuns-in-training who were closer to her own age treated her cruelly. Why did they dislike her so much Erin wondered, what have I done to be so offense to them? Then she realized her very existence offended them. They hated her because she was not Catholic, they hated her because she was pregnant. And they hated her just because she was there.

There was one exception however, Sister Mary Margaret. She

was a meek, sweet, kind and loving person. She believed all of God's children were special and she never uttered an unkind word. Even in her goodness, Sister Mary Margaret was also a target for the cruelty of the other nuns. Her face was terribly disfigured. Sister Mary Margaret was severely burned as a child. Her brother had thrown a can of petrol on a fire while she was standing close. When the petrol exploded, it did so in her face. As a result, her nose was partially gone and she had no lower lip. One eye drooped and was constantly weeping.

To a struggling family barely eking out a living from the land, a disfigured child was worthless, a female even more so. At least with a boy you could expect him to work the fields and be of some worth. As it was, she was one more mouth to feed and nobody would ever take her for a wife. So as a very frightened little girl she was placed in a Convent to do the Lord's work. Mary Margaret prayed daily that God would release her from her miserable existence and allow her to die. If it were not a guaranteed trip to hell, she would have murdered herself long ago. Sister Mary Margaret was kind to Erin whenever they were alone together. In front of the other nuns, Mary Margaret showed indifference toward Erin, for if she were kind to Erin in the presence of the other nuns, they both were summarily abused. From time to time, Sister Mary Margaret would bring Erin a piece of fruit or a biscuit from her own rations.

Chapter 7

One fateful day while clearing the dishes from the nun's meal, Erin picked up a piece of biscuit and quickly ate it. This time however, she was being watched by Sister Angelia who had intentionally left the morsel knowing Erin would consume it. Sister Angelia grabbed Erin's arm and spun her about. "You are a thief as well as a whore I see." Slapping Erin across the face, Sister Angelia knocked Erin to the floor. She retrieved her ever-present willow switch and began beating her. Erin curled up in the fetal position and covered her stomach with her arms to protect her unborn child. With her legs and head exposed, Sister Angelia had plenty of easy targets to expend her anger on. Erin received several blows across her face that would leave permanent scars. Her legs were bloody as well and the pain was almost unbearable. Even so, Erin continued to protect her stomach. Sister Angelia was in a frenzy, striking and cursing as if possessed.

Beneath Erin a growing puddle of blood was spreading. Erin cried out as the pain in her stomach was far worse than the whipping. She passed out. The other nuns held Sister Angelia back and said the child is in labor. Erin was carried to a closet and laid on a small cot. Sister Mary Margaret who acted as midwife was called. Sister Mary Margaret held her crucifix and began to pray. "Stop that you fool," yelled Sister Angelia, "God will not hear you praying for a Protestant whore." Sister Mary Margaret ignored her ranting and continued to pray while she administered to Erin.

Chapter 8

Knowing Erin had to be conscious during the delivery, Sister Mary Margaret pressed cold compresses to her face. Slowly, Erin regained consciousness. At first she did not understand what was happening, then Sister Mary Margaret whispered to her, "You are about to become a mother, the child is coming." But the child seemed to be in no great hurry to leave the comfort of his mother's womb. Being a tiny woman and this being her first pregnancy, Erin was experiencing a great deal of difficulty in birthing. She had lost a considerable amount of blood and was extremely weak. Several times it appeared she was losing the will to live and was on the doorstep of death. The nuns joked that they should alert the gravedigger and when they buried the mother, they would throw the bastard in with her. Sister Mary Margaret was determined to save both mother and child, praying continuously as she tenderly administered to Erin.

Sister Mary Margaret implored Sister Angelia to summon a physician. Sister Angelia refused, saying, "She is dying and a physician could do her little good. It is God's will." But Sister Mary Margaret refused to cease administering to the girl in her time of need. Erin's muscles were too weak to push the baby through the birth canal and both were close to death. Knowing there was precious little time left, Sister Mary Margaret reached inside and grasped the baby's head. This action invoked a piercing scream from Erin. The scream caused every muscle in Erin's body to react. It also gave the necessary push and with Sister Mary Margaret's gentle guidance the baby was born. With a slap on the bottom and a hardy howl, the baby boy entered the world. He was immediately wrapped in a towel and taken away. Erin had passed out during the birth, but when she regained consciousness, she asked for her baby. She was told the baby did not survive and was taken to be buried. Erin was extremely weak and decided she must join her child. From that time forward Erin refused to eat and would not accept any liquids. While the other nuns were content to let Erin suffer by herself, Mary Margaret made every effort to make her comfortable.

After three days and barely conscious, Erin laid on her cot and waited for the inevitable, when Sister Mary Margaret knelt by her bed and stroked Erin's hair. Erin opened her eyes and looked into the tearful eyes of the Sister. Mary Margaret spoke slightly above a whisper, "My child, God loves you as do I. You see the horrible disfigured face I live with. I would gladly trade my life for your baby were it in my power. I cannot understand what God has in store for you, though I am positive he wants you to live and to someday know your son." It took several minutes before what she had just heard registered in her semi-conscious mind. Erin's mouth opened though before she could speak, Sister Mary Margaret placed a finger on her lips and said, "Shush, what I am going to tell you, you must never repeat. If it were to be known that I have told you the truth, we would both be in grave danger. Do you swear by all that is holy you will forever keep this secret between the two of us and our heavenly Father?"

Erin's eyes were wide open as she nodded her head. Sister Mary Margaret lowered her voice to barely a whisper, "You had a healthy baby boy. He had red hair and blue eyes. He was beautiful. He was placed in an orphanage run by the church. You must have faith that someday you and your son will be together. To that end you must live, grow strong and prepare yourself for that day." Erin grasped the nun's hand and squeezed. Too weak to speak, she smiled at the nun as tears streamed down her face. Sister Mary Margaret rushed off to fetch some broth. After a few sips, Erin's weak body and deprived stomach rejected the broth and she began retching. Sister Mary Margaret held Erin as she rocked back and forth. After a few minutes the rejection of the broth subsided and Erin closed her eyes in sleep. Sister Mary Margaret washed Erin, put her in a clean gown and changed the bedding. Erin's fate was truly in God's hands. But God had a faithful servant in Mary Margaret and her devotion to the task at hand was unwavering.

A small sip at a time and Erin was able to keep the broth down. Too weak to leave the confines of the closet, a bucket served as receptacle for her body wastes. Gradually Erin was able to sit up and soon with Sister Mary Margaret's assistance she was able to stand. The effort was difficult and tiring. Day after day Sister Mary Margaret helped Erin to stand and after a few days Erin was able to take a few steps with her faithful companion's assistance. Erin graduated from broth to porridge and her strength slowly returned.

Chapter 9

A fortnight after the birth, Erin returned to her bed with the other inmates of the Convent. So happy to leave the confines of the closet, Erin was in good spirits. She was able to wander outside and even the experience of the outhouse was a blessing after the bucket. A few days later, quite early in the morning, Sister Mary Margaret shook Erin awake. "What is the matter?" she inquired. "They are taking you away this morning," she replied. "Where? Why?" Erin asked. "To the Magdalene Laundry in Cobh," the Sister whispered.

Shortly thereafter, Sister Angelia appeared with a smirk on her face. "We are finally getting rid of you," she hissed. As she had nothing to carry with her, Erin was taken down to a waiting vehicle and transported to her confinement in the Magdalene Laundry in the harbor town of Cobh on the eastern seaboard.

The laundry was an old run-down building in a shabby part of town. There was no garden, no trees, and the yard was merely a patch of weeds. There was a high fence surrounding the property, preventing any interaction from outsiders. The Sisters were housed on the second floor in reasonably comfortable rooms. In addition to their living quarters, there was a dining area, kitchen and a small chapel. The nuns had an inside toilet while the inmates used the outhouse behind the building. The inmates were housed on the first floor in one room. There were no real beds; pallets on the floor with straw filled bags were their sleeping arrangement, with one thin blanket per inmate. Erin was given a loose smock to wear, a towel and a piece of soap. There was a community hairbrush the inmates shared. Each inmate had a small table with one drawer for their Bible, rosary and prayer book, no other furnishings. There were hooks on the wall to hang their clothes while they slept.

Anything found beside their approved items would initiate a severe punishment. One time an inmate found a dead butterfly and hid it in her bible. When it dropped out while a Sister was going through her table, the inmate received several stripes on her thighs and was forced to eat the butterfly in place of her regular dinner.

Erin soon learned to keep her mouth shut and try to stay on the good side of the nuns. She toiled washing soiled linens from the nearby hospital. Blood, feces, urine and vomit impregnated the sheets. At first Erin was unable to touch the filthy sheets without gagging and retching. Each time she reacted to the soiled linens, she received a few stripes on her thighs. Eventually she became accustomed to the odor and was able to control her gag reflex. Each day was the same, nothing to look forward to, just the same routine, same food and same labour.

None of the other inmates came from a privileged family as did Erin. She also had a better education than the other inmates, as well as most of the nuns. Several of the inmates had mental problems. They often had fits of anger and would strike out at the nearest person. Erin was frequently the recipient of their outbursts. One inmate, Megan, was disfigured and quite unpleasant to look at. She hated Erin for her beauty and took every advantage to get Erin in trouble with the nuns. Each inmate had a washing tub. When the linens were sufficiently cleaned, they were placed in a rinsing tub. Before the linens went to drying, they were inspected by one of the nuns. Megan would sneak an unwashed sheet into Erin's rinsing tub. When the nun found it, Erin would get a caning and all of the items in the rinsing tub had to be re-washed. This was the torturous life of a lovely young lady whose only crime was one of the heart, compounded by trust and naïveté.

Chapter 10

The infant boy was sent to an orphanage near Dingle, County Kerry. The orphanage, as were most orphanages in Ireland, was run by the Catholic Church. The children ranged in age from infants to teens. Most of the children had been abandoned by their parents, too poor to feed and care for them. Occasionally, when their circumstances improved, a child would be reclaimed by his or her parents. Usually, it was a boy who had grown sufficiently to be some help on the farm. From time to time a child was sold to someone looking for cheap labour. Boys generally went to farming families to be field hands, and the girls to city dwellers to be domestics. In either case they were nothing more than slaves. When an infant arrived at the orphanage, it was placed in the care of one of the older girls. The infants were baptized and given names if their parents were known, that is if they came from Catholic stock. Babies left on the stoop of the orphanage usually had a note with name and religion attached. Protestant children were a rarity and were treated totally different. No good Catholic would consider wiping the arse of a Protestant bastard, so the infant was given to the care of a young girl who was in disfavor with the priest who ran the orphanage. Father Driscoll liked young girls; he liked them far more than his pastoral obligations would allow.

Sarah had been brought to the orphanage when she was five. Both of her parents were killed in an accident and with no other relatives willing to take her, she was sent to the orphanage. In about her eighth year, Father Driscoll began inviting Sarah into his office. He was very nice to the young girl and she enjoyed the attention. They would talk about her education and how she was getting along with the other children. Usually during these visits, the priest would give her a sweet biscuit or a piece of candy. Because all children are taught that a priest, being directly in touch with God was perfect and could do no wrong, when Father Driscoll had Sarah sit on his lap, she supposed it was all right. At first, she would just sit on his lap while they talked. When Sarah turned twelve, Father Driscoll asked her to come to his room. He said, now my child you are becoming a young lady, all grown up. Sarah blushed at the praise. Come here and give Father a hug. Sarah complied.

As they embraced, the priest began rubbing the young girl's buttocks. Sarah didn't think anything was wrong with this, after all, he was a priest. The priest sat in his chair and told Sarah to sit on his lap. She complied as she had done numerous times before. This time was different, for when she was seated, he ran his hand up between her legs and stroked her thighs. The priest began to breath heavily as he touched her private area. Sarah stiffened. "Relax my dear, I think you will enjoy this." As the priest started to slip his hand beneath her knickers, Sarah let out the most blood-curdling scream. The priest pushed Sarah off his lap and said, "Get out of here you little fool." Sarah ran from the room in tears.

One of the older girls pulled her aside and asked, "Did the old fool try to feel your muffin?" Sarah nodded. "He wanted to put his hand inside my knickers," she sobbed. "He has done that with every girl here at one time or another. One girl didn't stop him and then he tried to take her into his sleeping room. When she screamed and kicked at him, he let her go." Another girl spoke up, "The old wanker tries to touch every girl in the place. You must have scared the shite out of him when you screamed," one laughed. "I'll bet they heard you clear into town," another said.

Once she realized the other girls had been molested by Father Driscoll, Sarah calmed down. "I do not believe he will bother you again," one snickered, "not after that scream." One girl who had been listening quietly, started to sob. What's the matter with you Ilene? The little girl began crying. "He wanted to put his hand in my knickers," she whined. "Well did you let him?" one asked. The little girl nodded her head. "Why that old son of a bitch, and he tells us we are going to hell!"

Later, Sarah overheard three of the older boys talking. They were talking about her and Father Driscoll. "I wonder what the old wanker did to make her howl like that," said one. "That was a scream of pleasure," said another. "Probably gave the old fool a heart attack," said the third. Now Sarah was used to the antics of a bunch of pubescent boys. They were constantly trying to peek at the girls when they were dressing or preparing for a bath. On occasion, one of the oldest boys would expose themselves to the girls and make obscene offers.

Chapter 11

When the Protestant infant arrived at the orphanage, he was given to Sarah. "Keep the little bastard quiet," she was warned by the nuns. At first Sarah hated the infant. It seemed as soon as she cleaned his arse and changed his rag nappies, he would soil them again. Then she had to wash the filthy things. The child was always hungry and milk was limited. When she could get away with it, Sarah made a "sugar tit" out of a piece of cloth dipped in sugar or honey. The baby would suck on the cloth until it went to sleep. At the age of twelve years, Sarah was a surrogate mother. No longer was she able to play with the other children. Her time was totally devoted to taking care of the stupid little bastard. The other children, especially the older boys, would hold their noses and gasp whenever they came close to Sarah and the baby. "Gawd almighty, that little bastard stinks, smells worse than the shitter out back."

One day Sarah was holding the baby and it looked up at her and smiled. His tiny hand reached up for her face. At that moment Sarah's young heart opened up. She smiled back at the baby and said, "We are both outcasts, therefore we shall take care of each other, and to hell with the rest of them." The infant had not been officially named so Sarah decided to name him herself. Sarah believed God loved everyone even a bastard baby. Sarah though she should give him a name from the Bible. Perhaps God would be pleased. So, Sarah began calling the little fellow Thomas. A fine, strong name, one which she hoped God would approve of. From that day forward, Sarah became devoted to Thomas and loved him as if he were her little brother. Anyone who directed any abuse toward Thomas would find themselves confronted by Sarah. No longer would she tolerate any abuse verbal or otherwise from anyone.

On a particular day Sarah had left Thomas sleeping on her cot while she washed clothes. When she returned to check on the infant there were two boys passing Thomas back and forth. “Here, you take the bastard, no you take him.” They were having a merry time until Sarah arrived. One look at Sarah and the boy holding Thomas put him back on the cot. He had barely released the child when Sarah struck. She hit the boy in the nose with her fist then turned to the other and kicked him on his knee. When he bent over to grab his injured knee Sarah hit him with all her might. Both of the boys were older and bigger than Sarah. Both had been in scraps many times. But neither had ever been attacked by an angry mother before. They fled as rapidly as they could, yelling, “Hers mad as a box of frogs, she tried to kill us.” Later in the day, one of the nuns asked Sarah what had happened, that fighting would not be tolerated. Sarah looked at the nun and said, “I believe those wicked boys were scrapping over a top they were spinning.” Word spread that never again would the other children make Thomas a target of their sport.

Chapter 12

Thomas developed like any other child, under the guidance and protection of Sarah. Sarah taught little Thomas everything she could. She taught him the names of the birds and animals, told stories and read to him. Sarah taught Thomas to read and write and what arithmetic she knew. Thomas was a bright child who had an inquisitive mind and was eager to know everything. Sarah took Thomas with her when she attended class. The nuns taught the children basic reading and writing skills along with some math. It was a waste of time to teach them too much as they were destined to become laborers or servants. Some of the girls would marry older men who needed someone to keep house for them. Men came to the orphanage often looking for a suitable young woman. If they were successful, the orphanage received a sizeable donation. As for the girls, anything was better than living in the orphanage and they would be turned out once they reached the age of eighteen anyway. After living in a controlled environment for their entire lives, the prospect of being on their own was frightening. Some of the girls had jobs waiting as domestics or kitchen help, and boys were always needed, the bigger and stronger the faster they went.

When Thomas was approaching the age of six, Sarah was soon to turn eighteen. Sarah had developed into a beautiful young woman and would have no problem finding a husband from the surrounding area. But Sarah had other ideas. She had no intention of becoming the wife of a farmer or shopkeeper, washing his clothes, cooking his meal and having a baby a year. Sarah wanted more. She wanted an education, she wanted to take Thomas with her and be a family. But it was not to be. Sarah would be turned out when she became eighteen, but Thomas would stay in the orphanage. Sarah had been corresponding with a placement agency in Dublin and had interviews with three different families. One position was governess for a wealthy family with three small children. The other two were domestic positions. Sarah's experience with Thomas had instilled within her a profound love for children. She wanted to be a teacher, to show children there is far more to the world than their own back yard. To take them, as Dickens wrote, around the world on ships of paper. Sarah hoped that a position in Dublin would give her access to the great schools there. She imagined herself in a library with hundreds of books, even thousands. Her excitement turned to sorrow when she was informed Thomas would stay at the orphanage. In a couple of years, a strong lad like Thomas would be in demand and fetch a handsome donation. Sarah begged the nuns to allow her to stay and work at the orphanage, just so she would be with Thomas. The nuns said only Father Driscoll could make such a decision.

Sarah met with Father Driscoll and told him of her request. The priest put his elbows on his desk, put his hands together as if in prayer and rested his chin on his fingers. A sly smile crossed his face. After several minutes of silence, the priest spoke. "I shall approve of your request," then he paused. "On one condition," he said. "That you will become my personal assistant."

"What would that entail?" asked Sarah. "Taking care of my office, writing letters, overseeing the youngest children and most importantly, making me happy," he replied with a smile. Sarah's thoughts went back to a little girl of twelve who sat in this very office and the words Father Driscoll spoke then, "You want to make me happy, don't you Sarah?" Sarah got up and left the room without uttering a word. She went to her cot whereupon was a bag with every possession she had. She picked up the bag and went to find Thomas. Sarah explained to Thomas that she must leave. Although they had previously discussed this possibility, Sarah was the only family Thomas had known and he began to cry. "Don't be sad Thomas dear, I shall establish myself in Dublin and as soon as possible I will come for you. I will collect you as soon as I am able and we will never be separated again. My dear, dear little brother, how I love you. I shall miss you from the moment I walk through the door. I will write to you every week so you will know I am thinking of you." Sarah turned and walked away.

Chapter 13

True to her word, Sarah wrote every week. She had secured the governess position and was so pleased with her circumstances. The family was very kind to her and the children adored her. She was doing what she wanted most, teaching. The only sadness in her life was the separation from Thomas. The letters arrived faithfully each week for about three months then they stopped. Thomas worried that something had happened to Sarah. One day when Thomas was walking down the lane, he came upon the fellow that brought the mail. "Looking a bit sad today, are we?" he asked Thomas. Thomas told him Sarah had stopped writing and he missed her. The postman said, "No lad, you are mistaken, she writes every week, hasn't missed one since she left. In fact, I do believe I have mail addressed to you this very day."

"Well, why haven't I gotten any for weeks?" asked Thomas. "That I am unable to answer my boy, I just deliver the mail." Thomas asked, "Who do you give it to?"

"Why, to the Sister at the orphanage," he replied. "I understand all of the mail delivered is presented to the priest. He takes the mail directed to himself and then passes out the remainder." Thomas asked for his letter. "I'm sorry lad, my instructions are to deliver the mail to the home, and that is what I must do."

"But you're quite positive that there is one from Sarah for me?" asked Thomas eagerly. "Oh yes, here it is," and he held up an envelope. Thomas could see that it was Sarah's handwriting. He accompanied the postman back to the orphanage and watched as the packet of mail was given to one of the Sisters. Thomas waited for the mail to be disbursed. The inmate children rarely received any correspondence and none was handed out this day. Thomas knew he had a letter and wondered why he hadn't been given it. Thomas asked one of the Sisters if he had a letter. "The mail is in Father's office and if you had mail, he would have given it to you." Thomas went to see Father Driscoll. He didn't like the priest, none of the children did except one of the girls who he often saw going into the priest's office. Thomas was sure she was tattling on the other children. He knocked on the door and heard the priest say, "Enter." Father Driscoll was reading a letter when Thomas approached his desk. Father Driscoll looked up and saw who was standing before him. He hurriedly placed the pages back in an envelope. Thomas was positive that it was the same envelope he had seen earlier.

"Why are you bothering me, what do you want?" demanded Father Driscoll. "Please sir, I would like to have my letter from Sarah," replied Thomas. "You have no letter from anyone, now get out of my office."

"But sir, I know Sarah wrote me, the postman told me so," Thomas stated. "The fellow was mistaken, and never again argue with me," shouted the priest. "Now get out of here before I have one of the Sisters take the cane to you." The priest was a liar. Thomas walked out of the office and went to his cot. He removed his ragged coat from the hook, put his meager belongings into his pocket and walked out of the orphanage. He would go find Sarah and she would take care of him. There had been other children who ran away from the orphanage. They were always brought back. Anyone bringing back a runaway was given a reward. They were usually brought back bruised, battered and bloodied. Runaway orphans were fair game for the local toughs and drunkards. Since they were usually caught when trying to steal food, they were treated as criminals. Once recovered, the unfortunate child received his punishment. Father Driscoll himself would administer the whipping. He seemed to relish these events. The other children and the Sisters were required to watch. Each lash was accompanied by biblical verses, like "Spare the rod and spoil the child." Thomas knew that if he were to be caught and returned, his punishment would be more severe for he was a Protestant bastard. Father Driscoll would delight in beating a child destined for hell. Give him a taste of what eternity would be like. Thomas shuddered thinking of what could be in store for him.

Chapter 14

He had heard a couple of boys that had been caught and remembered what they had said. They had been noticed because they were strangers and everyone was on the lookout for a runaway. One must get far away from the orphanage without being noticed. So, Thomas proceeded with caution, diving into a hedgerow or behind a bush when anyone approached. Once, with a person approaching and finding no cover, Thomas climbed a tree and hid amongst the leaves. To his dismay, the traveler decided to stop under that particular tree and have his lunch. The fellow unwrapped some bread and cheese and slowly, ever so slowly, ate. Once he finished, he got up, stretched and turned and pissed on the tree trunk. By the time the fellow ambled down the lane, Thomas was stiff and could barely climb down to the ground. Thomas realized how hungry he was. He looked around hoping the fellow had dropped a few morsels of food, but there was none. For a split second he thought about returning to the orphanage, but quickly dispelled any such notion.

Thomas made his way past farmhouses and fields, detouring around when there was insufficient cover. He had never been this far from the orphanage before and if it were not for Sarah's teachings, he would have been terrified. As it was, he knew about the villages nearby and had a good idea of what he would encounter. As Thomas neared the first village, he knew it was the most dangerous. If they did not know of his escape, they would immediately recognize him as a stranger, a lad of six going on seven whom nobody would recognize was surely from the orphanage. Although hunger was announcing itself to his belly, Thomas skirted the town. When he heard someone approaching, he dived into the roadside bushes. A farmer driving a cart was hauling dried ears of corn to feed his cattle. As the cart passed by where Thomas was hidden, it hit a pothole in the road and several ears of corn fell from the cart. One of the ears rolled close to the bush where Thomas was concealed. Thomas's hand shot out and grabbed the ear of corn just as the farmer turned to see if any of his load had spilled. When he saw the ears of corn laying in the road he cursed, halted the pony and alighted and retrieved the ears. Thomas made himself a small as possible and hid the purloined ear of corn under his body so the bright yellow would not be seen as the farmer went by. After picking up the ears that had fallen from the cart, the farmer looked around to see if any had been missed. He looked directly at where Thomas was hiding, then turned and threw the errant ears of corn on the cart, climbed up to the seat and proceeded on his way.

Thomas began eating the corn; it was dry and hard but after a time in his mouth it softened sufficiently to be chewed. As the day progressed into gloaming, Thomas continued his journey into the unknown. Thomas had just passed a small farm house and was carefully sneaking past the milking shed when a voice called out, "You boy, what are you doing?" Thomas turned and saw a milk maid about Sarah's age standing with her hands on her hips. "Come here, right this instant," she commanded. Thomas hesitated, not knowing if he should start running or face the consequences of being caught. The choice was made for him when the girl started toward him. "Why you're just a little feller," she proclaimed. "What are you doing out here all alone?" Thomas stretched to his full height and replied, "Tis off to Dublin I am, to join me sister Sarah."

"Ha," said the girl, "Dublin is a far piece from here and it will take you many days before your journey ends." Thomas's facade of bravery crumbled and tears filled his eyes. "Are you going to nab me and take me back to the orphanage?" he asked. "Heavens no," replied the girl. "I myself was an inmate in that foul place. I remember Sarah and the baby she was charged with, are you him?"

"Aye, Sarah is me sister," he answered. "Na, she's no your sister, she had to care for you when you was brought to the orphanage."

"She is me sister," Thomas stated. "Well it's no matter to me," said the girl. "Come with me quickly before we are caught by the master." She led Thomas into the milking house and into a small room in the back. There were burlap sacks of grain and some harnesses in the room. "You can stay here for the night," she told Thomas. I will awaken you in the morning when I come out to milk the cows. The ornery old wanker never gets his arse out of bed until I'm finished with the chores and have his breakfast on the table. Are you hungry?" she inquired. "I'm so hungry I could eat the twelve apostles," Thomas answered. Laughing so hard she had tears in her eyes, she replied, "Stay here, I'll return shortly." She gave Thomas a drink of warm milk and she left carrying two pails of milk to the house. Thomas hid, not knowing his fate. Would the girl tell her master, would he be returned to the orphanage and a sure beating? After a bit the girl returned, and she had a piece of cloth wrapped around some cheese and bread. "In the morning before you leave, I will bring you a little more to take with you." Thomas ate every morsel, then lay down on the sacks and promptly fell asleep.

Early the next morning, long before it was light, Thomas was awakened by a noise in the milk house. Fearfully, he jumped up and peeked out the door and saw the cows coming in to be milked. Shortly thereafter, the girl entered the milk house. She handed Thomas a small package. "Here's some food for your journey, now you must leave before you are discovered." She embraced Thomas and kissed his cheeks. "When you find Sarah, tell her Marie Curley from the orphanage said hello." Thomas nodded, expressed his thanks and departed.

Chapter 15

Thomas walked all morning, hiding alongside the road when anyone approached. He feasted on the lunch Marie had given him. With his belly full, Thomas started down the road. In the late afternoon Thomas was so tired he needed to rest, so he propped himself up against an arbutus tree alongside the road. He did not intend to fall asleep but it happened. Thomas was startled by the approach of a vehicle. Quickly he climbed the tree as high as he dared. An old lorry pulled up by the tree and stopped. The three men who exited the truck were rough looking and had pistols in the waistband of their trousers. They kept looking back from the direction they came. One said, "I do believe we have lost the sons a bitches. Those bastards will remember this day," they laughed. Hearing the word bastard, Thomas flinched. In doing so he dislodged a small branch which fell at the feet of the three men. They drew their pistols and pointed them directly at Thomas. "Well, what do we have here?" one asked. Seeing it was but a small boy they lowered their weapons. "I think we have found us a fricken monkey," one offered. "Nay, it's a bloody squirrel, let's shoot the bugger and roast it for lunch."

"I ain't no monkey or no squirrel," the frightened boy said. "Come down lad, we mean you no harm." Slowly Thomas climbed down. Once on the ground Thomas found himself face to face with three very stern looking men. Fearing they would return him to the orphanage, Thomas started to run but in doing so had to come close to one man, who reached out and grabbed him. Holding Thomas by his collar, the man said, "Whoa there young fellow." Thomas kicked and struggled while the men laughed. "Another worthless Catholic cove," said another. "I am not, I'm a Protestant bastard," proclaimed Thomas. The men roared.

"Every Protestant is a bastard in this part of the country," said the fellow holding Thomas in the air. Gently setting him down, the man asked Thomas, "Wadda you doin' out here by yourself lad?"

"I ran away," replied Thomas. "Ran away from where?" inquired the second man. "The Catholic orphanage over by Dingle," answered Thomas. "Be damned if I ever heerd of anyone escapin' from those black witches," said the man. "You gotta name?" one asked. "Me name is Thomas," the boy answered. The third man had stood back by the truck and watched the road. He had a rifle in his hand and a pistol in his belt. Finally he spoke, "Come on fellas, we gotta get moving before someone comes along." One of the men told Thomas, "Get in the lorry, we'll give you a lift."

"Are we going to Dublin?" he inquired. "Hell no, we're heading back to Belfast," the man answered. "Let me go, I must find me sister in Dublin," Thomas yelled. "Another day perhaps, but not this one," he was told. With two men in the front and Thomas and the third man in the back of the lorry, they started off. The rocking of the lorry and the sound of the air rushing by soon put Thomas to sleep. When the lorry stopped several hours later, Thomas awakened. He looked around and found the lorry had been driven into a garage or shed. The men got out and began unloading guns and ammunition from under the tarp Thomas had been sleeping on. "Are you soldiers?" he asked. "We belong to the Irish Republican Army, so I suppose that makes us soldiers."

"How come you ain't wearin' no uniforms?" he inquired. "Cause we're secret soldiers," the fellow replied. "Who's you fightin'?" asked Thomas. "The bloody feckin Brits," came the reply. "Why?" asked Thomas. "Because the sons a bitches occupy our land and we aims to drive the bastards back across the sea to their feckin' queen. Now lad, you be quiet and stay out of the way, soon as we get the lorry unloaded, we gonna have some supper." The unloading took less than an hour and two of the men got in the truck with Thomas. The third man stayed behind to guard their booty, weapons stolen from a police station in central Ireland. "Now you listen and listen good young fellow, in the event we get stopped by the garda or any soldiers, your name is Thomas Flannery and I am your pa Phil Flannery, do you understand?" Thomas nodded. "Other than that, you don't say anything, you hear?"

"I hear," replied Thomas. The men drove for just a few minutes before pulling the truck behind a cottage. They went inside and were greeted by Phil's wife Teresa. "Who's the kid?" she asked her husband.

"We found him on the road down by Bunratty in County Clare. The little shite said he escaped from the orphanage over by Dingle," he replied. "He's such a wee lad, do you think it's true?" she asked. "Don't know, don't know any reason why it would na be. So what's for supper woman?" asked her husband. "What you get every night Phil, boiled cabbage and a rasher." He responded, "Fine, as long as there's plenty a stout to wash it down with." Teresa added, "Aye and there's plenty of fresh baked bread and butter."

So Thomas had the best meal he had ever eaten in his young life. It was the first time he had ever eaten at a table with adults, and never before a real family. After supper Teresa took Thomas aside and inquired when was the last time he had taken a bath. "A few weeks back I suppose," he replied. Then you're due for another she said. Teresa took Thomas in another room where there was a huge tub filled halfway with water. "Now take off those rags and get in," instructed Teresa. Having been raised in an orphanage where privacy was non-existent, modesty was not a concern to Thomas. He shed himself of his filthy clothing and climbed into the tub.

"I have never had first water before," said Thomas. "First water?" questioned Teresa. "Being the first one in clean water. Ususally there were several in the tub before my turn," replied Thomas. Teresa laughed, "From now on you will always have first water."

"Mercy me, I don't think I've ever seen a child as dirty as you, young man," and she proceeded to scrub. Teresa scrubbed Thomas until his skin was pink and raw. He thought she would never stop soaping his hair. "You've enough dirt in your ears to plant potatoes," she laughed. Finally, after what seemed like an eternity, Teresa handed Thomas a big towel. "Dry yourself while I go find some clothes for you. The rags you was a wearin' ain't fit for cleaning."

Teresa returned after a short absence. In her arms she carried clean trousers, a clean shirt, a pair of drawers, stockings and an almost new pair of boots. Thomas had never had such finery in his life. "How comes you got all these fine clothes?" he inquired. Teresa bowed her head for a moment then took a deep breath. "They were my son's," she quietly spoke. "Where is he?" asked Thomas. "He died some months back," Teresa answered. "Why?" asked Thomas. "Phil Jr. was playing with some other children and they found some kind of military device like a hand grenade. Little Phil tried to open it, he struck it several times with a rock then it exploded. Phil Jr. was just about your size, so I have plenty of clothes and even a fine, warm jacket for you."

"I'm real sorry about your son. Are you sure it's okay for me to wear his clothes?" Thomas asked her. "Oh yes, he would be proud for you to have them," Teresa said as she turned away. With her back to Thomas, she used her apron to wipe away the tears that flooded her eyes. Once composed, Teresa turned around and said, "Now it's off to bed with you." Not since Sarah left had Thomas been tucked in and kissed goodnight.

The next morning Thomas awoke to the smell of breakfast drifting from the kitchen. After getting his bearings and figuring out where he was, he got up and put on his new clothes. "Wash your face and hands before you sit at this table," Teresa admonished. Thomas obediently did as he was told. When he sat down, Thomas was amazed at all of the food. Breakfast at the orphanage consisted of porridge, occasionally with bread, even rarer with milk. Here before him was a feast the likes of which he had never dreamed. When Teresa handed Thomas his plate his eyes opened wide. "What is all this?" he asked. "Mercy me, tis just ordinary food," said Teresa. "I've never seen such as this before," Thomas exclaimed. "Whatcha got there," interjected Phil, "is an egg, a bit o ham, black and white pudding, boxty and a rasher of bacon. Now me missus herself made that jam so slather your bread good with it." Thomas ate until he was stuffed. Never had he eaten so well or been so full.

Teresa was overjoyed to see a young boy at the table once again. It was the first time since Phil Jr. died that she felt whole. Thomas bore a striking resemblance to young Phil, with red hair and blue eyes, of slender stature and within a month or two of being the same age. One difference was apparent to Teresa; Thomas was brighter and quite a bit more mature for his age than was her own son. Where Phil Jr. had been raised in a proper home with loving parents, Thomas grew up without a family, rejected and despised by everyone but Sarah. He learned to fend for himself and trust no one, except Sarah. For the next year Thomas was part of the Flannery family. Teresa grew to love him as her own. Thomas thrived in the loving atmosphere and developed into a fine boy. In school Thomas was eager to learn and excelled in all classes. What he didn't learn in school, Thomas was taught by Phil. He learned to fish and to snare rabbits, he learned to mend harnesses and to work with wood. He learned when to plant and when to harvest.

Chapter 16

Thomas also learned who his enemies were: the Catholics and the British. There were two Irelands, the Republic for the Papists and Northern Ireland for the Protestants, but Northern Ireland had been occupied by the British almost forever. It was high time they were driven out so a true Irishman could claim what was rightfully his. So in that light, Thomas learned of stealth, of deception, of thievery, of lying, and that which he became a master at, acting. Thomas could transform himself from a healthy lad into a sickly or crippled one in an instant. Being taught proper English from Sarah, Thomas could speak as if he were from the privileged class, or speak with the clipped talk of the lowers or working class, using slang and swear words liberally disbursed throughout every sentence. With these skills, Thomas was able to move about freely. Depending on the circumstances, when confronted by a British soldier he would either be respectful and emulate the local gentry, or from a distance become a ruffian and curse the English.

The boys of all ages threw rocks at the soldiers and if caught were guaranteed a good thrashing. Thomas was careful not to voice any disrespect toward the Queen for that could get you seriously hurt, even killed. Most of the British soldiers were young conscripts who came from the lower class. They had no particular loyalty to the crown, but despised the Irish far more than the gentry who subjugated them at home. Having been mistreated all of their lives, they were masters at mistreating others. Although their officers had instructed them not to use lethal force against unarmed civilians, the same officers turned their heads at the cruelty inflicted on the poor cove who was caught. Many a young Irish lad was left in the street with serious injuries. Broken bones were not uncommon and occasionally a beating resulted in death.

Chapter 17

Irish women never left their homes without at least one male escorting them. An Irish female of any age was fair game for the soldiers. Girls going to and from school always traveled in groups. Twice a day they ran the gauntlet. The soldiers were always waiting and ready for some sport. "Hey, red, I've got something for you," one would shout while the others laughed. The verbal abuse was nonstop with each soldier trying to outdo the other. Occasionally a soldier would expose himself along with filthy comments. The girls walked faster and the soldiers laughed harder. But the real danger came at night after the soldiers had downed a few pints. Any female unfortunate enough to encounter a group of rowdy soldiers would be subjected to more than just talk. They were assured of having hands all over their bodies. On rare occasion they were taken into a secluded area and raped. A soldier charged with sexual offenses would be severely punished by his commanding officer. The Brits tolerated a lot of abuse, but not rape. British officers knew well that the militants would extract revenge for defiling their women. Fathers, brothers, husbands, uncles, grandfathers, cousins and even neighbors were willing to die in order to get justice for the victim.

After one such incident, three British soldiers were found dead, and body parts had been placed at the front door of the commander's billet. That morning at muster, the garrison commandant spoke to the troops standing at attention. "This," he announced, "is what you can expect for violating an Irish female." Then he threw the severed parts in the dirt before the troops. "Three of our own died a most violent and painful death because of their stupidity. Since we cannot allow their deaths to go unpunished, many of you will be placed in peril as we seek out the perpetrators. From this day forward, any soldier guilty of rape will be shot. Our peaceful co-existence with the locals is fragile and we must not give them the reason to initiate a full-scale uprising."

That evening troops rounded up anyone they considered to be associated with the IRA. Phil Flannery was one of those detained. The commandant could not let the death of three of his men go unpunished, so three men, including Phil Flannery were summarily executed by firing squad. He did this as much to appease his own troops as a warning for the locals. His men were so outraged that their comrades had been treated so vilely for something as frivolous as raping an Irish woman, that they were talking about wholesale slaughter of the townspeople. Fearing a mutiny, the commandant did what he had to do.

There was outrage throughout the community and plans were being made to avenge the deaths of three good men. Thomas was especially affected by the loss of his surrogate father. Phil had been the only positive male role model in Thomas's life and the manner of his death would have a profound effect on Thomas forever. Sadness soon gave way to bitterness, and hate filled the void where once love and respect had resided. Thomas listened to the older men discuss ways to avenge the death of their friends. From some there were cautions: "If we kill a few Brits, they will kill more of us, and they have a never-ending supply of soldiers, we are but few. There are already enough widows and orphans, we cannot continue to give the soldiers excuses to kill our men." Others however were not so mindful of the consequences; they wanted to make the English pay dearly just for being in Ireland.

A meeting was held at the usual place, the home of Phil and Teresa. Teresa sat in the room with the men, although normally women were excluded from such meetings. Being her home there was little they would do, so Teresa was allowed to stay. "So, what can we do to hurt them the most without drawing attention to ourselves?" Several men offered suggestions, however they were the usual tactics of hit and run, do a little damage and wait for the Brits to retaliate. Finally, Teresa spoke up. "Phil told me that the cost of keeping troops here is a drain on the English economy and there are many who would have them return to their own soil."

"What's your point, woman?" one of the men asked. "Phil told me he was trying to figure out how to disrupt the supplies coming from England," Teresa answered. "One of his thoughts was to rob the quartermaster when he brought the troops pay."

"And did he say how this could be done?" Teresa was asked. "From what I remember, the money arrives by ship with the other supplies and replacement soldiers. The ship anchors in Belfast Lough off Newtownabby. The soldiers are put ashore in longboats along with any passengers, and crew members on liberty. The ship's Captain usually goes ashore later to have dinner with the local dignitaries, returning after midnight. While ashore, the Captain arranges for the dock workers to unload the ship and receives instructions on the transfer of the money. There is far more than just the soldiers' pay, there is money for the operation of the city and salaries for municipal employees. The second day the ship is brought to the city docks where it is unloaded. Once the money has been taken ashore, it is received by an officer and escort. It is taken to the bank and from there it is dispersed. A driver, an officer and usually two other soldiers escort the payroll."

One of the men spoke up, "There is no way we can get the money before it gets to the bank, and the lorry has but a short distance to travel to the garrison, and we would never get away with trying to snatch it along the way."

"Phil must have been dreaming," voiced one of the men. Teresa spoke up, "Phil said the weakness in the whole procedure was the first night the ship arrived, after the Captain went ashore and before he returned. Phil said there was only a skeleton crew aboard and most of them would be drunk. They do not even keep lookouts when at anchor."

"The whole idea is crazy," someone offered. "Yes, so crazy it might just work," said another. "And how in the hell are we supposed to get aboard the ship?" someone asked. "While the women are at the fantail of the ship attracting the sailors, the men could climb up the anchor chain and hide. But even if we successfully boarded the ship and found the money, it would be both in gold coin and pound sterling and too heavy to get away with."

"We don't need to get away with it, we merely drop it over the side," said Teresa. "That will disrupt the distribution of the soldiers' pay and the money will be waiting for us at the bottom of the bay when we can recover it at our leisure. The success of the mission will depend on our being able to drop the money box over the side without alerting the crew."

"That's a pretty iffy proposition," someone interjected. "Suppose, just suppose the sailors were distracted," Teresa offered. "Distracted by what?" someone asked. "What is the one thing on the sailor's minds when they have been to sea," asked Teresa. "Whiskey and women," someone laughingly said. "Exactly," agreed Teresa. "But how do we get aboard the ship?" someone asked. "Four men could row up to the ship with several of our lassies and some special whiskey. The men cling to the anchor chain and out of sight, the girls go aboard and feed the whiskey to the sailors. When the sailors pass out, the men drop the money chests over the side and everyone leaves. When the Captain leaves the ship, he gives a ration of rum to the crew left on board. It isn't enough to get them all drunk, so before we get off the ship we break into the room where they store the barrels of rum. It will appear as though the sailors did it. When the Captain and crew return, there will be no evidence we were ever there. They will not discover the missing money until they fetch it to deliver to the garrison. It will have disappeared into thin air. Can you imagine the repercussions for the Captain and the crew? Since the money is locked away once it is brought on board and probably not even looked at until it is to be delivered, no one will know when it was taken or by whom."

In an instant and without another spoken word, a woman became a leader in the resistance. Every man in the room recognized Teresa had her husband's leadership abilities and his quick mind. It was as if Phil was speaking through his wife. Practically every man in the room was a laborer, they were uneducated and for the most part illiterate. Few could read or write and none had the practical mind of Teresa. She had listened to Phil so often that she thought as he did. So, the plan was adopted and men were given assignments. The first order of business was a small boat, of which there were several that would be sufficient. Teresa enlisted several volunteers who would go aboard the ship and do whatever necessary to distract the sailors. Not only were they willing to offer their bodies to the enemy, they were prepared to give their lives.

Chapter 18

Not too far from the village lived an old hag. No one knew what her name was or where she came from. She had just always been there, living in a cave a few miles out of town. She was a healer whose life was dedicated to the study of plants, leaves, roots and all of the fungi that grew in the forests. She knew what combinations produced what results. What potion would heal a cough, what lotion or salve would heal a burn. She knew how to set a broken bone, and remove an infected tooth, the best time to get married and the time to seed the fields. She was a midwife as well and those too poor to hire a doctor availed themselves of her services. In payment she would accept anything, from food to trinkets. Although she preferred to be alone with her plants and the critters she lived with, her heart was always open to those in need. By the lower class she was revered and loved, by the gentry she was nothing more than a crazy old witch. The local physician had tried several times to have her run out of town without success. The local clergy had also made attempts to drive her away for she practiced the ancient ways of the Druids. Her knowledge was far more extensive than just the healing arts. She could cast a spell, create a love potion, induce an abortion in a foolish young girl, mix a concoction that would immediately put one to sleep, and with certain mushrooms and crushed beetles make a deadly poison.

Now Teresa needed her help. If the plan were to work, the sailors would need to pass out quickly, though not before all had had a drink, and hopefully before any of the females had to submit to the sailors. As Teresa explained her plight, the old woman frowned and slowly shook her head. Fearing rejection, Teresa asked what was the matter. The old woman replied, "I have a potion that would work, however when added to alcohol its effect becomes much stronger and can produce death. Usually, it is added to tea or water or a juice of some sort. I must test it with the whisky to adjust it for the proper effect. And I must use the same whisky the sailors will be drinking for the alcoholic content will change the potency. If the sailors die the whole plan would be exposed and the repercussions would be devastating for the entire village."

"What shall we do," asked Teresa? "First, I need some of the whisky, then I need some lads who would be willing to test the potion." Laughingly Teresa said, "The lads will be no problem and practically every man in town is brewing poteen."

"All of the whisky must come from the same batch," the old crone replied. "Time is of the essence so we must begin immediately," said Teresa. "How many lads do you need?" The old woman replied, "Three or four will do."

Chapter 19

A meeting was hastily called and Teresa explained the situation. When volunteers were mentioned almost every hand in the room shot up. "We need lads who are about the same age as the sailors," Teresa voiced. So, the older men were excluded; two young and two middle-aged men were chosen to test the brew. Paddy Delany said he had two gallons of poteen that he would donate to the cause. The next day four men and several jugs of poteen arrived at the cave. After the old woman had mixed several cups of differing strengths, the men all drank. Almost immediately Derek Connelly dropped to the ground. "That one's too strong," the old woman said. It must not act too quickly for we want all of the sailors to drink before they are affected. Should one or two drop too quickly the others may not drink. It should take ten to fifteen minutes before it takes effect, that will insure all have had a chance to drink." She had just uttered the last word when Timothy O'Rouke dropped to the ground. "Again, too strong," muttered the old woman. Several minutes passed before Sean Clancy fell to the ground. "It has been over ten minutes, so that one will do. Now we must wait and see how long before they wake up."

"Might I have another sip while we wait?" asked young Barry McCracken. "Nay, nay," said the old woman, "I may need your help with these lads. We don't know for sure how they will react when they come to." At that she gave Barry a drink which she said would nullify the potion. For the better part of an hour Barry and the old woman waited. Finally, Sean Clancy began to stir. He sat up groggy and with a splitting headache. Almost immediately he began to vomit. The old woman smiled. "That's a little something I added so those scoundrels would suffer a bit," she mused. She then gave Sean a drink which would set him right again. Timothy O'Rouke came to a few minutes later and was given the antidote. It took almost two hours before Derek Connelly came to.

The old woman prepared seven liters of the special brew and one liter of plain poteen for the women. When the men departed, they did so with a special warning from the old woman. "Be sure and tell the women taking part in this adventure to drink only from the one bottle. The effect of the potion on the women will be greater than the men due to their smaller bodies and lighter weight."

So the plan was put into action. A week later the English ship arrived and anchored in the bay. Just like clockwork the soldiers and passengers were taken ashore. Next the sailors granted liberty were taken ashore. Soon Captain Elija Goodall and the officers left the ship. Teresa, the women and men who were taking part in the raid waited in a cove on the opposite side of the bay. In the dark and with the ship between them and the town, there was less chance they would be seen. Teresa instructed the women to rinse their mouths with poteen and spill a bit on their clothes. They would appear as if they had been drinking and could deny any offers of drink by saying they were already drunk and that if they drank anymore, they wouldn't be able to properly satisfy the sailors. Should anyone insist they drink, it was imperative they drink from the proper bottle.

Chapter 20

When they heard ten bells from the ship the group departed, slowly rowing toward the ship so as not to create any noise. When they reached the anchor chain, the men climbed high enough so as not to be seen by anyone walking around the rail. One would have to peer over the side in order to see them. The women rowed toward the rear of the ship and began singing. Soon sailors were hanging over the side yelling down to the women in the boat. "What are you gals doing out here in a rowboat?" asked one sailor. "We heard you sailors knew how to please a woman and we came out to see if it's true."

Oh, it's true," said one sailor as he dropped a ladder over the side. "Climb up here and we'll show you." The girls tied the boat to the end of the ladder and climbed up, each holding a bottle of whisky. They had no sooner climbed over the railing when they were each grabbed by a sailor. "Slow down fellows, we intend to stay awhile and have a party." The girls held out the bottles and one said, "I heard you sailors could put away the whiskey."

"Let me show you," said one as he took a long pull on a bottle. "Don't hog it all," said another as he took the bottle and tipped it to his mouth. The girls paid their attention to the sailors who had taken a drink, hoping the others would follow suit. Before long all of the sailors had a drink and put their hands all over the women, one giving a kiss while another felt a breast. Soon it was all the women could do to keep their clothes from being ripped off. "Take it easy honey, there is plenty of time. Where do you fellows sleep?"

"In hammocks down below love," was the response. "Then let's go there where we can get comfortable." The girls paired off with sailors while the others drank and said, "Don't take too long, we want a turn too." By the time the girls and their escorts reached the living quarters, three of the four sailors had already dropped to the deck. "Have another drink sweets," said the girl with the lone standing sailor. He tipped back the bottle and before it touched his lips he dropped.

The women went topside and found all of the sailors passed out. One ran to the bow of the ship and called the waiting fellows aboard. The men headed to the location of the ship's storeroom where the chests of money were kept. The door was locked so the hinges were removed. They removed the chests and placed them in the passageway. The door was replaced and there was no evidence that it had been taken off. With two men on each chest, they were taken topside and dropped off the port side of the ship where they could not be seen from the village. After the third chest had been dropped overboard, the men located the rum barrels. The barrel that had been in use during the voyage was almost empty so they dumped it out. Knocking the bung from one of the full barrels, they rolled it on its side as if cups were being filled. They removed two buckets of rum from the barrel and dumped them over the side.

All of the raiding party except one climbed down the ladder into the rowboat. The remaining man pulled up the ladder and stowed it in its normal place. Then he ran to the bow and climbed down the anchor chain and into the waiting rowboat. None of the whisky bottles were left behind nor was any evidence that women had been aboard the ship. The entire operation had taken less than one hour and other than a few bruises on breasts and buttocks, none of the women had been violated. The row back across the bay was uneventful although tense. As soon as the rowboat was secured, the members of the raiding party disbursed to their respective homes.

Chapter 21

The Captain and officers returned to the ship about 0100 hours. When his longboat pulled alongside the ship, the Captain expected a ladder to be waiting, but there was none. "Ahoy, ahoy, where's the Captain's ladder?" yelled one of the junior officers. No reply. The Captain, full of good food and a little tipsy from some twenty-year old cognac was furious. He ordered one of the crew to fire his pistol in the air. Shortly thereafter a head appeared over the rail. "Lower the ladder you idiot," yelled the Captain. As the Captain set foot on the deck, he saw sailors lying about moaning, some in the process of vomiting on the deck. "I want every one of these sons a bitches flogged at muster in the morning," he told his executive officer. "Aye Captain, it shall be done." The Captain went to his cabin and promptly fell asleep. The executive officer toured the ship and eventually came upon the room where the rum was stored. It was obvious what had occurred. The crew had broken into the rum supply and gotten drunk.

The name of every seaman aboard was written in the ship's log. By reveille at 0600 the entire crew was back aboard ship. Muster was at 0700. The seamen who were aboard the ship the previous night stood apart from their usual places in their respective divisions. The Officer of the Day called the senior seaman to step forward. "Can you explain to the Captain what occurred on this vessel last night and explain your behavior?" The senior seaman, whose name was Brown said, "I'm not quite sure sir. A group of women were aboard and the next thing I know is that it's morning and I'm sick."

"Are you out of your mind, sailor?" the officer shouted. "Where in the hell are the women? How did they get on and off the ship? There was no ladder over the side when we returned from shore. Did these women fly to the ship, then fly back to shore?" he shouted. "You men broke into the rum locker and got drunk, and for that you shall be flogged for the entire crew to witness. Getting drunk on duty will not be tolerated under any circumstances, and for you to stand there and lie will give you a few extra lashes."

"Please sir," the sailor responded, "we did not break into the rum locker and there were women who rowed a prow to the stern of the ship last evening. We thought they were whores and did lower a ladder and allowed them aboard. They brought whiskey with them and after a drink we all passed out." The Captain spoke up, "I've heard enough of this dribble, flog them." The men were taken one by one to the main mast. There they were stripped of their shirts and their hands tied over their heads to the mast. The senior boatswain's mate wielded the cat o' nine tails. A vicious form of punishment, the whip consisted of nine strips of leather about six feet long. The first foot and a half or so had been wrapped with leather strips to form the handle. Each of the tips had a small piece of metal attached. When lashed, the metal bit into the flesh and the pain inflicted was most great.

The first seaman led to the mast was shaking like a leaf. He was young, no more than twenty and he had never experienced a lashing. In order to maintain the respect of his mates, a sailor must receive his punishment without crying out. As the first lash tore into his flesh, the sailor gasped, though he made no other sound. As the cat o' nine tails connected time and time again the sailor began moaning. His eyes rolled back in their sockets and he slumped on his tethered hands. When the lashing was done, a bucket of seawater was thrown on his back. The cool water brought the sailor back to his senses and the salt burned into the wounds like a hot poker. The lad was cut free and with assistance was walked back into line.

The next sailor to be flogged was even younger, perhaps no more than sixteen or seventeen. He was crying and had to be assisted to the mast. From the first to the last lash, the boy cried louder, and by the time he had received all ten, he was blubbering incoherently. When taken back to stand in line he could not and crumpled to the deck. One by one, the remaining sailors were taken to the mast and received their punishment. One older seaman had received the lash before for when his shirt was torn from his body there were scars visible from a prior experience with the "cat".

The final man was Brown. Being senior, his punishment was more severe. Even though he had spoken the truth about the prior night's events, he was not believed for there was no evidence of any others being aboard the ship. Brown silently took twelve lashes before he passed out. The punishment was halted and a bucket of seawater thrown on the unconscious man, for what good is a lashing when the recipient is unable to feel it? A second bucket was necessary before Brown came to. The final three lashes were applied and he was cut free. Brown could barely stand, but managed to remain upright. The Captain walked up to Brown and said, "Do you have a different tale to tell now?"

"No sir," replied Brown, "I have spoken the truth." The Captain then asked, "Would another series of lashings loosen your tongue and help you to be truthful?"

"No sir, I do not lie." While the Captain pondered this response, a Lieutenant Baldwinn addressed the Captain, "Permission to speak, sir." The Captain nodded his head ever so slightly. The Lieutenant spoke, "Captain I have had seaman Brown under my command for several voyages. He is a first-rate sailor and has never been a behavioral problem. Seaman Brown has always performed admirably and I have never known him to be untruthful."

"Then how do you explain the disgraceful actions of this man and the men under his command?" demanded the Captain. "I cannot answer that at this time," replied the Lieutenant, "and respectfully request the Captain allow me to conduct an investigation into this affair." The Captain mulled this over for several minutes while silence prevailed on the ship, with the exception of the sobbing of the youngest of the men flogged. "Very well Lieutenant," the Captain replied, "you may have your investigation, though the punishment will be far more severe should you discover further wrong doing. Am I understood?"

"Yes, sir," said the Lieutenant as he saluted his Captain. The Officer of the Day dismissed the crew and instructed them to hoist anchors and prepare to dock for unloading. The crew dispersed to their respective stations and the ship sailed to the dock and was secured with lines. Precisely at noon, a convoy consisting of a large wagon pulled by four horses, three smaller wagons with single horse, two officers mounted and twelve soldiers with rifles marching in formation approached. As they neared the ship, the Officer of the Day ordered a crewmember to alert the Captain that the Paymaster had arrived. The Paymaster was escorted aboard and received by the Captain in his cabin.

Chapter 22

"Good to see you Earl," said the Captain. Earl Foxworth was an Army Field Officer with the rank of Colonel. He and Captain Goodall had known each other for many years and each had a profound respect for the other. "Understand you had a spot of problem last evening Elija?" inquired the Colonel. "Nasty business Earl," said the Captain. "The entire watch crew got falling down drunk while I was ashore. Seems they broke into the rum locker and helped themselves. Never in all my years at sea has such blatant disregard of responsibility occurred. I know the lads like to get frisky after being at sea but never have I seen so many men involved. From time to time a rogue in the crew will screw up but never a whole watch crew. They were so shit faced that couldn't even give a straight story about what happened. Some cock and bull about a boat load of women coming aboard and getting them all drunk. Never heard the likes of it before."

"That does sound strange Elija, you've always had a well-disciplined bunch of lads." The Captain sighed, "I just pray that it's an anomaly and will never happen again." A pounding on the door and shouts of "Captain, Captain!" broke the silence. "For the love of God, what in the hell is going on?" said the startled Captain. "Enter," he shouted. The cabin door burst open and a junior lieutenant rushed inside. "It, is gone, it's gone, he babbled. "What's gone, you damn fool?" demanded the Captain. Catching his breath, the Lieutenant responded, "The money Captain. Gone, all gone."

"What are you saying, Lieutenant?" the Captain demanded. "The vault room is empty, there are no money chests, there is nothing in the room," replied the Lieutenant as he regained his composure. "Impossible," said the Captain. I possess the only key and I personally saw the money chests put in the vault room, and I myself locked and padlocked the door. The key has been in my possession until this very morning when I handed it to you, Lieutenant." The Lieutenant stood mute before the two senior officers. "Come along Colonel, I'll get to the bottom of this," said the Captain as he pushed back his chair and briskly stood. They rushed down the passageway to the lower deck where the vault room was. The door was standing open and the room was empty. The seamen who were to unload the money chests and the soldiers who were to guard it during transport all stood at attention.

The red-faced Captain turned to the Lieutenant, as the veins in his forehead became most prominent and spittle sprang forth from his mouth as he spoke, and said, "I want this vessel searched from stem to stern, no one is to leave the ship until I allow it, is that perfectly clear?" The Lieutenant saluted and answered, "Perfectly clear sir" and he turned to issue orders to the waiting seamen. As the search got underway, the Captain and the Colonel proceeded to the bridge to observe the activity. Shortly after their arrival on the bridge, they were joined by Lieutenant Baldwinn. "Sir something very peculiar is going on. I interviewed each of the seamen aboard the ship last night individually. Their stories are almost identical in every respect."

"What is your point?" asked the Captain. "The point sir, is that if the men were indeed drunk, how could their version of last night's events be so similar? Drunk men do not normally have their wits about them and would be unable to fabricate such an elaborate and ridiculous tale. Even their descriptions of the women are the same. Since I believe the men were drugged with the whisky brought aboard by the women, they were sober when the women appeared. Therefore, I feel quite positive the men could identify the women involved. Furthermore sir, I have inspected the vault door and I feel certain the door was removed from its hinges to gain access. There are pry marks barely visible that someone had attempted to conceal."

"Lieutenant Baldwinn, if you are correct then the money chests were stolen by the Irish." The officer responded, "That is my belief sir."

"Baldwinn, I want you to go ashore and arrange a meeting with Governor Hastings," ordered the Captain. "Aye, aye sir, I will depart immediately." The Captain added, "And Baldwinn, do not discuss this meeting with anyone, and that is an order."

"Yes sir," replied Lt. Baldwinn.

Chapter 23

With two soldiers as escorts, Lieutenant Baldwinn proceeded to the Governor's office located on the first floor of his mansion. The Governor was a huge man fond of self-indulgence. He surrounded himself with a following of "yes men" who stumbled over one another trying to gain favor for themselves. Hastings was appointed Governor of the English-held corner of northern Ireland not because he possessed any outstanding merits, but due to the accidental overhearing of a plot to harm a senior official in the Kings court. In reality a low-level official and bumbling ass-kisser, the governorship was as much to exile him as it was a reward. Hastings lived a life of luxury in his private domain. He was gluttonous, cruel, narcissistic and histrionic. As Governor he was quick to judge and equally as quick to punish. He derived great pleasure in floggings and hangings, often enjoying a hearty meal and copious amounts of wine while some poor bugger's back was laid open or he swung by the neck. Hastings was a sadistic sexual deviant whose proclivities leaned toward very young children, children of either sex. And in a country where the indigenous occupants were considered less than human, Hastings had little problem finding victims. It was as simple as sending a few of his lackeys out in the countryside to snatch any child unfortunate enough to be left unguarded.

As Lieutenant Baldwinn entered the Governor's office he felt immediate revulsion. The greatly obese Governor sat behind a grand desk in the largest chair the Lieutenant had ever seen. Although clothed in expensive style, the front of the Governor's blouse was stained with food that had never quite made the journey from the plate to his cavernous mouth. "Quickly, quickly Lieutenant, I am quite occupied. What is the purpose of this unscheduled visit?"

"I beg your pardon my Lord. I bring respects from Captain Goodall, who wishes to arrange a meeting with your Lordship on a very urgent matter." The Governor inquired, "What is this urgent matter?"

"I am not at liberty to discuss it my Lord, I am merely to arrange a meeting between my Captain and yourself." The Governor shouted, "I order you to give me a reason for the meeting!"

"Your Lordship, I am a naval officer and take orders only from my commanding officer. I mean no disrespect sir, but am unable to say more." The Governor's huge face turned bright red and he looked as though it would burst. "Go fetch your Captain immediately," he yelled, "and I shall see you flogged for your insolence. Now get out of my office!" The Lieutenant retreated immediately and returned to his ship where he proceeded directly to the bridge. "The Governor requests your presence immediately," he reported to his Captain. "Did the fat bastard phrase it so gently, Lieutenant?" the Captain asked as his face broke into a wide grin. "Perhaps not quite so civilly sir," he answered. The Captain, accompanied by Colonel Foxworth arrived at the Governor's office shortly thereafter.

Chapter 24

Casting aside all pleasantries, the Governor glared at the Captain and the Colonel for several seconds before demanding the purpose of this unwanted meeting. When told the chests containing all monies to fund the local government and pay both the civil servants and military personnel had disappeared, the Governor jumped to his feet, erupting in a tirade of blasphemy and threats. “You incompetent son of a bitch, you were responsible for the safe delivery of my money. I’ll have you and your entire crew hanged. Arrest him Colonel.” Colonel Foxworth spoke, “Your Lordship, as senior military officer of the garrison protecting this colony, I will allow no harm to befall the Captain or his crew until such time as the truth is revealed. The ship will be quarantined and no crewmember will be allowed ashore except as I direct. There is evidence suggesting that locals are responsible for the disappearance of the money chests, although at this time we do not know how they accomplished it.”

“You intend to usurp my authority do you?” the Governor spat. “Governor, the money is entrusted to first the Navy and then the Army until it is delivered to the local bank. It was stolen on our watch and it is our responsibility to recover it. The Governor sat down and his demeanor slowly changed. His red face faded into its normal pink shade and with his elbows on the desk, he put his chubby hands together to form a steeple in front of his face. Very softly he said, “You have 48 hours to recover my money. Should you fail I assure you heads will roll.”

“Then we had better get started Captain,” said the Colonel as he made a mocking bow to the Governor. As they walked back to where the ship was tied, Colonel Foxworth said, “Elija, with your permission I would like Lieutenant Baldwinn assigned to my command as I investigate."

"As you wish Earl. He thinks he's on to something it seems," answered the Captain. "Yes, it is interesting that all of the men seemed to be sober until the mystery women appeared. I've no doubt that they had their daily ration of rum but these lads can handle far more than a ration before they are as drunk as they seemed to be. And they all seem to describe the same women. I believe we should have every woman in the village between the age of sixteen and fifty rounded up. We will show them to the men individually and see if the same women are picked out. Tell Baldwinn to get his men ready to go ashore tomorrow at 0700 and meet me in front of the drill compound."

Chapter 25

The following morning forty-seven women stood in a line in the center of the drill compound. One by one the sailors walked down the line and from time to time pointed at one woman or another. After they had viewed the women on display, only one was pointed out by every sailor...Teresa Flannery! Since the sailors were only positive about Teresa, the other women were permitted to leave. Teresa had planned well, as the other women who participated in the adventure we all farm girls from the surrounding countryside. Her mistake was herself. Teresa was taken into an office and questioned. When she refused to admit to any participation in the boarding of the ship, the officer questioning her punched her in the stomach. Teresa doubled over gasping for air and vomited on the floor. Her head was pulled back by her hair and she was smacked several times across her face. Nose and lip bleeding, Teresa maintained her silence. I'm already dead she thought, I'll not give the British swine the satisfaction of hearing me beg, and I will die before I betray my mates.

Teresa was taken out to the drill grounds and secured to a post. The Corporal who normally welded the whip had never whipped a female before. He was a dull lad, somewhat lacking in his wits. He took no great pleasure in whipping men, although it didn't appear to bother him either. But this was different; a woman would scream, beg and plead. Her flesh was soft and would yield quickly to the lash. As her clothing fell from her body, he would see her naked and he felt the excitement in his groin. The first lash tore through her blouse and undergarment. It cut diagonally from her right shoulder to her left hip. The second lash formed an "X" on her back. The Corporal in his excitement got careless and the third lash cut across the back of Teresa's head. Cut to the bone, the wound gushed blood. There was an unintended effect of the blow, as it had rendered Teresa unconscious, unable to feel the pain being inflicted on her body. When there was no cry for mercy blow after blow, the Corporal struck with a frenzy, lash after lash after lash. He continued to swing his whip long after her spirit had departed Teresa's broken body.

"Where does she live?" asked the officer in charge. "On the edge of town in the yellow place," someone offered. "Take her home and burn it down." And so, the only parents he had ever known were together again, and once more eleven-year-old Thomas (with no last name) was an orphan. Thomas grieved as any eleven-year-old would; he cried, he cursed, he railed at the unfairness of life, he lamented the loss of those who treated him so well. But he realized he was on his own once more. Without a home, without a family, without anyone or anything, Thomas was alone.

Chapter 26

He slept in a hayloft, as the only home he knew had been burned to the ground. Thomas survived by stealing; he lifted fruit from the market place stalls and when desperate, ate the grain that farmers set out for their stock. He stole clothes from the wash lines and bathed in the river. Thomas was becoming self-sufficient but he also was becoming careless. One day while trying to lift the purse of a passerby, Thomas was nabbed. A soldier saw him steal the purse and quickly grabbed him. "Where do you live?" he demanded. "Nowhere," replied Thomas, "I have no home."

"Where are your parents?" the soldier asked, and "I have no family," was the answer. "So, you have no place to live and no family to provide for you, therefore you are a vagabond and a thief." Thomas remained silent. "We've a place for rascals like yourself," said the soldier and he dragged Thomas to the barracks office. The duty officer began the paperwork to incarcerate Thomas as a criminal. "What is your name lad?" he inquired. "My name is Thomas."

"What is your family name?" he demanded. "What is that?" asked Thomas. "Everyone has both a first name and a last name. What is your last name?"

"I don't know, Thomas answered. "I must completely fill out the paperwork and I must have a last name." He looked up at the soldier who had delivered Thomas. "What is your name, Private?" he asked. "Private First-Class Clarence Arnold," he replied. "Good enough," said the duty officer, "the scoundrel is now Thomas Arnold."

"He's not my boy," protested the Private. "No matter," said the duty officer, "He'll be off to England on the next ship and you'll never see him again." Thomas was placed in a cell with several other boys, all older than he. When the evening meal was served, Thomas had barely received his plate when it was grabbed by one of the older boys. Thomas learned very quickly that when he was handed a meal to shove as much in his mouth as it would hold, for the remainder would fill someone else's belly.

Chapter 27

It was two weeks before a ship took Thomas to England. Upon arriving in Liverpool, he was taken to the Reform School for Wayward Boys. There were about sixty lads in the Reform School, but only six were Irish. Thomas was immediately singled out for his bright red hair and freckled face. "Another mick bastard we have to feed," said the headmaster. "Well, this little son of a bitch will earn his keep or starve. I'll be damned if I'll give him food when true English lads are hungry." While the English boys had cots with rope netting and straw, like the other Irish, Thomas was relegated to sleeping on the cold floor. He was given a well-worn blanket with many holes in it, and told if he lost it, it would not be replaced. The next morning breakfast was served, porridge and a crust of bread. When Thomas got up to the server, he was given a piece of bread and told the porridge was gone. Thomas could see in the pot that there was sufficient porridge to serve several more but he was denied any.

Soon thereafter Thomas was approached by a boy nearing the age of fourteen. He took Thomas aside and told him of the workings of the Reform School. First of all, any Irish were considered to be lower than dogs and would be treated accordingly. The primary income which sustained the institution was derived from begging. Every inmate was sent out daily to beg, steal or by any other means return with at least four shillings. Those who came back with less received no meal, those who came back empty handed were rewarded with a beating. Since the Irish were not considered human, every possible obstacle was placed before them, the first being the mark. All Irish inmates received a tattoo on the right foot. It was a crude tattoo of a four-leaf clover. As none of the inmates wore, or even owned shoes, the mark made it difficult to beg, for to the average Englishman Irish were scum. The few Irish lads learned to blacken their feet with coal dust as soon as they were sent out each morning. Those with bright red hair such as Thomas soon learned to keep their heads covered. Soot on the face hid the freckles and learning to speak with a Cockney accent helped them achieve their daily goal. Some of the lads earned money by performing sexual acts on men in alleyways. The Irish refused to engage in this pursuit saying no true Irishman would stoop so low.

Thomas soon learned that even if he returned in the evening with a pound or more it didn't matter. He was still denied a full ration of food and was continually abused by both the staff and the other inmates. Since it did him no good to return with more than a pound, Thomas began hiding any extra funds he acquired. Since he was considered the enemy by the Brits, Thomas had no hesitation taking whatever he could lay his hands upon. He became quite skillful at picking pockets and lifting jewelry off the passing gentry. On one day Thomas was walking along looking for a mark when a girl came running toward him. She was being chased by several people including a Bobby blowing his whistle. "Stop thief," they shouted as they pursued the girl. As she approached, Thomas could see the frightened girl was losing ground to her pursuers. He sprang forth and grabbed her arm. "Come with me quickly," he shouted. They darted down an alley and through a courtyard, out the other side and down more alleys. Doubling back, they soon were behind their pursuers. They reached a park and hid amongst the bushes.

"Why were they chasing you?" Thomas asked. The girl held out her hand and displayed five shillings. "The man gave me this to put his hand inside my knickers, but I ran when he gave me the money." During their escape they had run through several puddles and Thomas noticed on her left foot was a tattoo exactly like his. He wiped the grime off his foot and showed the girl his tattoo. "Why are you here?" inquired Thomas. "A Brit soldier grabbed me and was putting his hand under my blouse and I kicked him between his legs," she replied. "He told the garda that I approached him and when he refused to pay me for a feel, I assaulted him. Because he was an Englishman, I was sent here to go to court. The court ordered me to pay a fine of ten pounds. I had no money and was sent to the workhouse. The master gave me a choice, I could pay for my keep one way or another. Visit him at night or pay two shillings a day for my food. I am let out each morning and have to return by nightfall. The master said if I failed to bring at least two shillings each day he would use me himself and then sell me on the street."

"What of your family?" inquired Thomas. "I have none," the girl replied softly. My father died when I was a small child, I really have no memory of him. Me mum married a man with two sons. From the onset, the two boys took over. They ordered my mum and me around and even hit us both. They complained about everything and their father just sat back and watched. If either of us complained, he would laugh. The two boys could do no wrong. They cursed me, pulled my hair and called me names. I did very well in school and they did poorly. Every time I received a good report, they hit me and threw dirt at me. Both me and my mum were no better than slaves. I was just in the way it seemed. A few years back, when I returned home from school and was changing clothes, the two boys decided they wanted to see me undressed. When one decided to help me remove my clothes, I hit him with a heavy vase and split his head open. Shortly thereafter my mother and her husband came home, and the boys said I attacked them without provocation. Mum was completely controlled and terrified of her husband and the two boys. I was told to get out and never return. My mum cried and begged for me to stay. All to no avail and I was turned out."

"What did you do?" inquired Thomas. "At first, I just wandered about. Then I met a girl I knew from school. When I told her what had happened, she hid me in the shed behind her house. She brought me food and a change of clothes. I stayed there for about a fortnight, then one day her father came to the shed and found me sleeping. He called me a vagabond and ordered me off his property. After that I slept under a bridge or in an old barn on the edge of town. Occasionally, I would come across one of my former neighbors. They too were afraid of Mum's husband and the boys. One lady gave me several coins from her purse and I bought food with it. Then one day I met one of my teachers on the street. She took me home and I had a hot bath. I could not stay long for her family was due back. She gave me a bundle and I left. When I opened the bundle, there was bread and cheese and a piece of bacon. After that I wandered around some more. Sometimes I was so hungry I would snatch a piece of fruit from a vender. Other times I would beg coins from strangers."

"So, what are you called?" asked Thomas. "My name is Eloise Monahan, and I've recently turned thirteen," she replied. Thomas said, "I think we are about the same age. I am an orphan and not quite sure of my birth date, but I believe it is about the same as yours." When she asked his name and his only response was, "Thomas," she inquired, "Just Thomas, no family name?" Thomas just shrugged.

Instantly, a friendship was formed. With no family and no friends, they were like two peas in a pod. Although both of them were usually suspicious of everyone, they immediately trusted each other. "How would you like to be partners?" asked Thomas. "We could work together and two is safer than one. I will help you if you will help me."

"I will, replied Eloise. "What are your plans?" she asked. "I want to leave this fecking town and live in the country," said Thomas. "That sounds wonderful," replied Eloise. "How about you Eloise, what do you want to do?" She answered, "I really never made any plans other than getting through each day. But the country sounds lovely. Would you allow me to go with you Thomas?" He replied, "We are partners ain't we?"

"How much do we need to get away?" she asked? "I really don't know," he answered. "Nor do I know how long it will take to accumulate enough. So every day, we will hide a bit until we have enough. If either of us should come up short, the other would make it up." They each spit on their palms and shook hands. "Now we must find us a place where we can keep our stash," said Eloise. "I have one," replied Thomas with a smile. Thomas took Eloise to a park and showed her a large cobblestone by a fountain. The stone lifted up with a little effort. Beneath was a hole about a foot deep and about six inches across. Eloise looked in the hole while Thomas stood watch. There were a couple of bills, a few coins and some jewelry in the bottom. "Hurry, put the stone back, someone is coming," whispered Thomas. Eloise replaced the stone and stood just as a couple came strolling in view. As the couple approached, Eloise stepped toward them. "Please sir, have you a spare coin for a poor girl?" she asked. "Get away from us, filthy ragamuffin," he muttered. "Oh Franklin, she looks hungry," said the woman. "I is ma'am, we both is," nodding toward Thomas. The man relented and threw a couple of coins on the ground. "Thank you, sir, may you be blessed." The man snorted and the couple moved on. "What a wanker," said Thomas when they were out of hearing distance.

Chapter 28

Thomas and Eloise worked as a team. Eloise would entice some dandy into an alley on the pretense of being a street tramp, then as soon as she received the money and the mark had dropped his pants around his ankles, she took off. Once the mark began the chase, Thomas would intervene. The mark would find himself tripped over a piece of wood or "accidently" run into by Thomas. In any event, Eloise would escape. A couple of times Thomas received a thorough thrashing, but was never suspected of complicity in the action. Both Thomas and Eloise made enough money to appease their keepers, and add a little to their private stash. They talked about escaping their confinement and returning to Ireland and living in the country. But the news they received on the streets was not promising. Neither had any family left in Ireland save Sarah, and they knew not where she was or how to find her. There was talk of hunger and illness in Ireland and the Brits made it even worse. Escaping from one hell only to enter another was not a feasible option. They had heard of America where the Irish were treated well and there was plenty of food, so that became their goal. They would save enough for passage to America. Once there they would find work and live free. For three years Thomas and Eloise continued to scam, scheme and steal. Their stash grew to the point the hole was almost full.

One day after a close encounter, Thomas and Eloise retreated to the park bushes. Eloise was crying and Thomas asked what had happened. "The bugger grabbed me boob and pinched it something awful," she said through her tears. Eloise lifted her blouse and under garment, exposing her left breast. Below the nipple was a large bruise. Thomas stared at the exposed breast. It was the first time he had seen one on a developed young woman. He just stared. Eloise looked at Thomas and her crying ceased. She covered herself and asked, "Have you never seen a girl's titty before?" Thomas blushed and shook his head, "I seen naked girls at the orphanage, but they was little girls, they didn't have any titties." Eloise took that as a compliment and leaned over and kissed Thomas on the cheek. "Well someday I may let you have a proper look," she laughed. All Thomas could do was nod his head! As it was getting late in the day, they would have to hurry or be late. Being late meant no supper and probably a good thrashing as well.

They met every morning at the clock tower and each day worked a different part of town, though there were areas they did not venture into. Street children were in their element in some areas while in others they would stand out and the coppers would run them off.

Thomas kept a watchful eye on Eloise as they worked the streets. One day Eloise picked a dandy who appeared to have money. As she approached him, she motioned toward the alley and gave him a smile and a wink. The fellow looked around then followed her. Once they were in the darkness of the alley, the man grabbed her. "I know what you are up to my little bird, and it won't work." He laughed and said, "Iffin you was cleaner I might take a chance, but I'll settle for a feel or two. And if you try anything, I will beat you well and drag your arse to the nearest copper." Eloise was terrified, afraid to cry out for the coppers would never take her side. She began to cry. "That won't help you little twit," he snarled as he slapped her across the face. Eloise began to struggle and the man drew back his fist, then he felt the blade enter below his rib cage. As he dropped to his knees, Thomas grabbed Eloise by the arm and pulled her away. They began running. Behind them they could hear someone yelling, "Murder, murder." Soon the shrill sound of a Bobbie's whistle sounded. Their only advantage was their knowledge of every side street, walkway and alley in the area. It took them several minutes until they had out maneuvered those pursuing them. Hiding in some bushes Eloise sobbed, "They have our descriptions, they know we are beggars. They know where to find us, what shall we do?"

Fully aware that they were unable to return to their respective places of confinement, Thomas said, "Come with me," and led Eloise to a section of town that had previously been off-limits to them. They stayed in the shadows for the likes of them were rarely seen and not wanted in this part of town. As darkness fell around them, Thomas and Eloise hid under a small bridge. Pondering their options, Thomas finally said, "I must go recover the money we have hidden. If we are to be accepted in this part of town, we must change our appearance to look like we belong here. We must have shoes and nicer clothes. Stay here out of sight until I return," he instructed Eloise. "Please hurry?" she asked. Looking to make sure the coast was clear, Thomas left. To Eloise it seemed he would never return, and for a fleeting moment she wondered if Thomas had abandoned her. Then she heard a rustle in the leaves above the bridge and Thomas appeared.

Eloise was so relieved to see him, she gave Thomas a hug and kissed his cheek. "We have far more money than I thought," Thomas told her. "The pieces of jewelry I took to the pawn broker and purchased this," and handed Eloise a small bundle. When opened, she saw it contained a piece of soap, a length of ribbon, a comb and a pair of scissors. "We must make ourselves clean and as presentable as possible," said Thomas. "We must be careful of the way we talk and how we act if we are not to attract attention," interjected Eloise. The water flowing beneath the bridge was shallow and very cold, but the cleansing had to be.

Before removing her clothing, she shook her finger at Thomas and said, "Don't you dare be looking now." Stepping into the cold water, Eloise immediately began to shiver. She scrubbed and scrubbed until her skin was pink and the cold water no longer was a bother. She worked on her hair for the longest time. Having no means to wash her hair and nothing to comb it with for so long, her hair was tangled and filthy.

Eloise turned and asked Thomas, "Have you been looking?" Thomas told her no. "Not even a little peek? Wouldn't you like to have a look?" Turning red he stammered, "Well yeah, but you told me not to." She said, "Well, I shouldn't mind a quick look if you wanted to." Eloise was standing hip deep in the water when Thomas turned around. Although he had seen young girls undressed at the orphanage, Eloise was a maturing young woman and much more developed than Thomas had ever seen.

Smiling, Eloise stepped out of the water and picking up an article of clothing, she covered herself. "Thomas please, I need your help, my hair is tangled so badly." Ever so gently, Thomas separated the tangles in Eloise's hair. He was pleased to see her hair was red like his. Eloise's hair was a dark, deep red, almost maroon, while Thomas's was a much lighter colour. She had dark eyebrows and brown eyes, while Thomas had blue eyes and his eyebrows were colorless. Thomas removed the tangles and soon the comb was gliding through her hair. Eloise slowly turned around and Thomas knew he was in love. She had huge freckles across her nose and on her cheeks beneath her eyes. Eloise took a step back and asked, "Well, what do you think?"

"You are beautiful," Thomas stammered. He admired her, stepping back and nodding his head. Never before had he seen anyone so lovely, and suddenly there was a strange feeling in his trousers. "Now don't just stand there gawking," scolded Eloise, "your turn." She dried herself as best she could with her clothes and dressed. Thomas removed his tattered and ragged clothes, entered the water and began washing himself. Not since he lived with the Flannery's had Thomas been so clean, though the filth did not submit to the soap and scrubbing easily. After leaving the water and putting on his clothes, Eloise took over. "Now it's time to do something with your hair," she instructed. Thomas sat on a rock while Eloise wielded the scissors. "You must look like a proper young gentleman," she commented as she took a snip here and there. "When I'm finished you must trim the back of my hair Thomas." When he told her he'd never cut hair before, she replied, "It isn't difficult. Just cut a small amount at a time and you will do fine." So, Thomas and Eloise were clean but their clothes were not.

"Now we must rid ourselves of these clothes, and we must have stockings and shoes for these wretched tattoos will give us away immediately," stated Eloise. "I'll go get some clothes," replied Thomas. "No, I will go," said Eloise. "You could not pick clothes for me, though I can pick yours. I will leave as soon as the morning traffic begins. The more people on the streets, the less likely anyone will pay attention to me." So, Eloise took money and set out to purchase clothes. The first vendor she sought out sold used shoes. Eloise purchased a pair and immediately put them on. Next Eloise located an old crone pushing a cart piled high with used clothing. They retreated into an alleyway and Eloise picked out two pair of stockings, two each of knickers, petticoats, dresses, a shawl, a coat and a parasol. Dressing behind the old woman's cart, she threw her old rags in a nearby dustbin. The old woman looked at the transformed girl and said, "Dearie, you sure looks different," and handed Eloise a silk handkerchief. "A gift me lovely," said the old woman. "Now I need a satchel in which to carry my things," Eloise said to herself. Hearing this, the old woman dug through her pile and produced a small suitcase. "For only six pence love," she said as she held out the suitcase. "It will serve my purpose," said Eloise as she paid the woman.

Chapter 29

With her new clothes, Eloise became a proper young lady. She walked with poise and appeared as if she were from an upper-class family. Men doffed their caps as she passed and ladies smiled at her. When a Bobby approached Eloise tensed up, for fear of the law had been instilled in her. But the Bobby touched the brim of his helmet and smiled as he passed. Eloise nodded and smiled in return. When three sailors came walking toward her, they all knuckled their foreheads and smiled. Eloise nodded once again. It seemed she had accomplished her goal, for she fit in. Now she needed to turn her attention to the needs of Thomas.

It wasn't long before she saw a cart piled with men's clothing being pushed her way. She picked out several items for Thomas, including two pair of trousers, suspenders, drawers, stockings, two shirts and a cap. But no shoes or boots. Next Eloise went into a pawnshop and purchased a pair of high-top shoes and a jacket. Eloise returned with her purchases to the bridge where Thomas waited. Before putting on his new clothes, he had to re-wash his feet for he had been pacing back and forth waiting for Eloise to return.

"From now on, we are brother and sister from Devonshire visiting relatives here," stated Eloise. Thomas had relinquished his role of leader to Eloise. Being clean with proper clothing brought out the strength Eloise formerly had. Thomas was in love and happy to follow Eloise's bidding. "It's time for our debut," said Eloise and the pair walked out into the busy street. They entered a pub and ordered fish and chips and a pint of ale. The meal was the best they had had in months, and it was all they could manage to eat properly rather than wolf it down. Twice Eloise cautioned Thomas to slow down. "We no longer must hurry through our meals. Watch the others while they eat and do as they do. And Thomas dear, you must use the napkin and not the sleeve of your shirt to wipe your mouth." It took some time, but soon Thomas was able to control his hunger and his manners. Eloise reminded Thomas of Sarah always teaching him.

Chapter 30

They left the pub and window-shopped most of the afternoon. As it was nearing time for the evening meal, Eloise said, "We should get a room at an inn before it is too late." Walking toward the outskirts of town, they came upon a small cottage with a sign in the window, 'Room to Let'. "Do you think it is by the night or for lease? Let's ask." They approached the door and knocked. An old woman opened the door and asked, "What do you want?"

"We saw your sign and wanted to know if the room was to let for the night." The old woman asked, "Have you money?" Eloise replied, "We have sufficient for our needs."

"Show me, show me your money," the woman demanded. "Exactly how much do you require for a room for my brother and myself?" Eloise asked. "Brother huh? How many beds, dearie?"

"One bed and a pallet or a couch will do," said Thomas. "Well then, it will be six shillings," said the old crone. Thomas paid her and they were ushered into the house. "Would you be wanting something to eat?" the old woman asked. "That would be lovely," replied Eloise. "Would you prefer fowl, fish or chops?" she asked. "I should like chops," said Thomas. "I would prefer fowl," said Eloise. "Very well, give me money and I will go to the butcher's before he closes." Thomas looked at Eloise and shrugged. He gave the woman a pound note and said, "Bring some ale as well."

The old woman left and soon returned with the meats and ale. Thomas noted there were far more chops than one could eat and several pints of ale. "Was there money left over?" he inquired. "Not a penny," the old woman replied. The meal was quite good and the old woman had purchased sufficient for her to enjoy it with them. The ale had loosened the old woman's tongue, and she rambled on about her life and how miserable she was. Seems she had been engaged to a soldier who never returned after being sent to Ireland. She accused those murdering Irish with ruining her life. "If I ever get my hands on an Irishman, I will strangle the bastard," she proclaimed. "Unlikely you will run across any Irish in this part of town, my dear," said Eloise. "I should hope not, they are animals and not fit to be in the presence of a proper English woman." Soon all retired for the evening.

"Turn your head away while I get ready for bed Thomas. No peeking." With a sly grin Thomas placed his hands over his face, though he left his fingers spread a bit.

Chapter 31

Next morning the old woman greeted them with tea and biscuits. "Would you be wanting breakfast, love?" she asked Eloise. "Shirred eggs and toast would be fine," she replied. "Very well dearie, give me money and I will hasten down to the market and purchase some eggs and bread." Entering the room, Thomas overheard the exchange and gave the woman five shillings. "Tis not enough," she stated. "Purchase what you can for that amount, woman. I'll not be taken advantage of twice." The old woman wrapped a shawl around her head and left.

After breakfast, Thomas and Eloise left the old lady's home and began walking around town. They strolled through the numerous parks and looked in all the shop windows. Nearing noon, they began looking for a pub to have lunch in. They wandered toward the docks when they saw a large crowd gathered. As they approached, they heard a man shouting as the people crowded around him. They walked close enough to listen. "Passage to America, cheap fare to America, seek your fortune in America," he shouted. Thomas and Eloise moved closer. "The ship leaves in two days, get your passage before it's too late. The next voyage will not be for three months so secure your passage now. The sooner you are in America the sooner you will find your fortune. Free land and plenty of work to be had. Get your passage now."

"How much?" someone asked. "First Class passage is only fifty pounds per person. Children at half price. Fine cabins available in Second Class for only thirty pounds."

"Too much," someone said. The pitchman was undaunted. "There's always room in steerage. Plenty of room left in steerage at only ten pounds for adults and three pounds for children."

Thomas asked a gentleman standing nearby, "What is steerage, sir?"

"Not a place for young people of your class," he replied. "It's for the poorest of the poor. A great many of those in steerage do not make it to the final destination. Stay clear of steerage young fellow."

Now steerage on a ship was in the hold, the bottom of the ship. With no portholes, poor ventilation and only candles for light, the hold was never designed for human habitation. Therefore, there were no proper toilets, merely buckets to use. Although there were a few hammocks, most had to bed on rough planks or decking. As the hold was one huge area, there was no privacy. Men, women and children were crammed together in a dark, damp environment that was home to all sorts of vermin and huge rats. The only food for those in the hold was soup and stale bread. Any food left over from those in cabins on the upper decks was put in a pot with water and called soup. Occasionally, a few scraps of meat found their way into the mixture. That and leftover bread, usually quite stale, was the only fare for the weeks of confinement in the hold. Water was delivered to those in steerage once every morning. Barely enough for drinking, there was none for washing bodies or clothing. The close quarters, the buckets of human waste and the stifling heat created an almost unbearable odor. The stench was so bad, the crew would keep the hatch covers closed so the stench didn't rise up through them. The hatches were the only openings for fresh air, so for the inmates in the hold it was a constant battle to keep them open. Those in steerage were not permitted above deck.

This left Thomas and Eloise in a dilemma. They could not afford a berth in one of the cabins and steerage seemed out of the question. They left the docks to ponder their options.

Chapter 32

As they strolled through a park, they observed an older couple. The old lady had fallen and her husband was attempting to help her up, though being of advanced age, he was unsuccessful. "May we be of service sir?" asked Thomas. "Please young man, I am unable to help the Missus get up." Thomas being a strong chap, easily lifted the old woman and helped her to a nearby bench. Eloise immediately straightened the woman's clothing and comforted her. Not in possession of a handkerchief, Eloise used the hem of her dress to dry the lady's eyes. With her hands she smoothed the woman's hair and straightened her bonnet. The old gentleman stood by watching as his wife was administered to. When she regained her composure, the woman took Eloise by both hands and kissed them. "I am ever so grateful, young miss." Looking up at her husband, she said, "Elrod reward these fine young people." The old fellow took a ten-pound note from his pocket and offered it to Thomas. As Thomas extended his hand to collect the note, Eloise spoke up, "Sir, we cannot accept payment for rendering assistance to someone in need." Thomas pulled back his hand with a perplexed expression on his face. The man pocketed his money, looked at his wife and shrugged his shoulders. "Very well then," the woman said. Looking at Thomas and Eloise she asked, "Then you will dine with us this evening at our home. What are your names?"

"I am Eloise and my brother is Thomas." The lady asked, "Do you live close by?" After a bit of hesitation, Eloise said they were just visiting the city. "And where are you from, dearie?" Eloise looked at Thomas for help, so he stammered, "The country up north." The old fellow raised an eyebrow and furrowed his brow. "My name is Sir Elrod Rooney and my dear wife is called Charlotte. We look forward to having you dine with us." After giving them directions to their home, the old couple departed.

Chapter 33

Thomas looked at Eloise and said, "At least we shall receive a free meal." Eloise admonished, "Hush up Thomas. One should not expect to be rewarded for doing a kind deed. I should expect any normal person would have done just as we did." Having been properly chastised, Thomas said, "You are right, I am glad we could be of service to the old ones."

"That's better," Eloise said with a smile. "Now let us be on our way, we have several hours to decide our next move." The next few hours were spent walking around and looking in the shop windows. "What time are we supposed to present ourselves for supper?" Thomas asked Eloise. "Half six is what the old woman said."

"Well, we best be heading in that direction for it is just now approaching six," he replied. "Thomas, we are sure to be asked questions over supper. We must be prepared to explain our circumstances." Thomas answered, "I have it all sorted out. Just follow my lead."

At the appointed time Thomas and Eloise arrived at the home of the Rooney's. It was a rather large house in a better part of town, an area neither of them had been in before. Thomas lifted then dropped the knocker and they waited. It was some time before the old fellow opened the door and ushered them in. "Please excuse the delay. Our man and his woman left us a fortnight back and we have been unable to find replacements. Being eighty years old, I move rather slowly these days." He took them into the parlor and gave them each a glass of sherry. "Charlotte is a fine, fine woman and excels in the kitchen. Even so, she too is getting up in years and is unable to do everything she once did."

Just as they had finished their sherry, the old woman announced supper was ready. Thomas and Eloise were taken into the dining room. Eloise asked, “How are you feeling after that tumble Ma’am”?

“Ah, I was bit wooly headed and I’ve a couple of tender spots on me bum,” she laughed. “Otherwise, I’m quite grand.”

The table held a feast; there was boiled beef, chops and a fowl, with greens, carrots, cabbage and turnips and mashed potatoes with gravy. Red wine was poured for everyone and Elrod proposed a toast. “To my darling wife and to kind strangers.”

Thomas and Eloise tried to emulate the way their hosts were eating, for they had never before dined in such opulent surroundings. Cut a piece of meat, lay the knife down, then eat. Thomas had always held a fork in one hand and the knife in another, and both did the dinner dance at once.

As the meal progressed, Charlotte began her questions. “Where do you live?” Thomas answered, “Our parents died a few years back and we lived with our Auntie. Aunt Millie died a few months ago. Unbeknownst to us, Aunt Millie had run out of money. She was living on credit. When she passed, the creditors took possession of everything. We were turned out of the house with our clothes and little else. We each had a small savings and have been using it while we decide what to do.”

“Brilliant,” Elrod exclaimed. “You are without a home and we are without domestics. How would you like to live here and be in our employ? Lad, you would do the outside work and run errands. Room and board and two pounds a week. Now Eloise would help in the kitchen, do the laundry and keep the house up. She would get room and board and one pound a week. How does that sound?”

“Nay,” said Thomas, “that will not do sir, that will not do.” Elrod asked, “Why what do you mean?” Thomas answered, “Eloise would be working just as hard as me, therefore she should deserve the same pay.”

“But we never pay the women as much as the men,” Elrod professed. “My sister and I are equals,” said Thomas, “and must be paid the same amount.” Elrod Looked at Charlotte and said, “Either we pay the lad less or the girl more to make them equal. What do you say, love?”

“Elrod you are a scoundrel. Either way you would be paying them less than the ones before them,” Charlotte announced. “Alright, alright, no more of the matter, two pounds each. Eloise your room will be on the second floor and Thomas you should be quite comfortable in a room downstairs. It is a bit smaller, but young fellows do not require as much room as do the ladies. We are all in agreement then."

"I will show Eloise her room," voiced Charlotte, "while you take Thomas to his quarters, my dear."

Chapter 34

The following morning Thomas retrieved their meager possessions from under the bridge where the bundle had been hidden, while Eloise helped prepare breakfast. “Elrod is quite picky my dear,” Charlotte told Eloise. “He must have two soft boiled eggs, a rasher of bacon, and toast with orange marmalade precisely at eight each morning. By that time, he has already had his tea and is ready for food.” Charlotte showed Eloise exactly how Elrod liked his meal. It was a joy for Eloise; for the first time she felt needed and useful. Charlotte walked her through her new responsibilities, pointing out in which order she preferred things done. Laundry was to be done every Friday, shopping for groceries Monday morning. The farmers bring fresh produce and meats to town on the weekend, so by Monday it is laid out for sale,” she explained. “Therefore, we must be to market first thing Monday morning immediately after we prepare Elrod’s breakfast.”

Elrod showed Thomas the furnace and coal bin. “You must be vigilant when the coal is delivered Thomas. I fear that coal fellow counts a bit on the short side. I certainly do not mind paying for the coal but I refuse to be taken advantage of. Something you will learn later in life my boy, as soon as you accumulate a bit of wealth, there are those ready to relieve you of it. The tools to care for the garden and yard are in the shed out back.” Eloise and Thomas, both being quick of mind, learned their responsibilities in a very short time.

Before long, Eloise was handling almost all of the cooking, even Elrod’s breakfast. She did most of the cleaning and was rapidly learning how her mistress preferred the laundry to be done. The one area where Charlotte maintained strict control was Monday’s shopping. Charlotte was most picky when purchasing meat, be it beef, pork, fish or fowl.

She was well known in the marketplace and the vendors gave her a wide berth. Charlotte would only purchase the finest cuts of meat and only the freshest fish and fowls. A vendor who tried to slip one past her was in for a tongue-lashing he would never forget.

Thomas enjoyed working in the yard. He liked the physical exertion and working outdoors. He trimmed the bushes and kept the lawn just the way Elrod showed him. He kept the leaves raked up and the walks clear whenever it snowed. The better part of a year had passed when one night after supper and the dish washing was complete, Charlotte asked Eloise to fetch Thomas and meet them in the parlor. Once everyone was present, Charlotte began, "It has been a very long time since we have attended the theater. Elrod and I plan to go Saturday next and would like you two to go with us."

"Oh! My," said Eloise, "I have never been to the theater in my life."

"Nor have I," Thomas spoke up. "Well, would you care to join us?" asked Elrod. Eloise blushed and looked at Thomas. "We would be out of place, for we could not dress properly for such an occasion." Charlotte smiled, "We thought that might be the case, but there is plenty of time to get you the proper attire. I will take you shopping in the morning Eloise and we will find you a magnificent dress. Elrod will take Thomas to his tailor and fix him up with a fine suit of clothes. Would you like to go with us?"

"Yes, yes," they both voiced in unison. "Very well, it is settled." Eloise took Thomas aside. "You must take a proper bath tonight Thomas, and wear only your cleanest clothes. Though we are not gentry, we must not embarrass these fine people."

Chapter 35

The next morning off they went on their shopping spree. Thomas was fitted with a charcoal coloured suit with silk lapels, white shirt, a white vest, a black cummerbund, a pair of black shoes and silk stockings. Next came a fine top hat. Other than a cap, Thomas had never before worn a real hat. Decked out in his new clothes, Thomas felt like a millionaire.

Charlotte took Eloise to a milliner's and proceeded to fit her with a bonnet. After trying at least a dozen, Charlotte gave up. "We will first find you a dress then shop for a bonnet." So off to the dressmakers they went. Eloise tried on several dresses, each one acceptable to her, but not to Charlotte. "One must not purchase a dress hastily," she said. "We must find one that compliments your beautiful red hair and fair complexion." Finally, Charlotte narrowed the selection down to two dresses, trying first one then the other, then back to the first, then again to the second. Finally, Charlotte said, "This is enough, we will take them both." The selection of petticoats, knickers, stockings, and a pair of high-top button-up shoes went far quicker than selecting a dress. "Now let us return to the milliner's and select a bonnet or two." This time they were successful in purchasing a bonnet for each dress.

"Why am I fitted with two outfits?" asked Eloise. "A lady must never ever wear the same outfit twice in public. No one cares about what a gentleman wears but everyone notices what a lady is wearing." Eloise did not understand, they were only going to the theater once. But Charlotte left no room for disagreement. They met up at a restaurant for supper for it was too late to return home and cook. They would collect their purchases in two days after alterations had been done and everything had been pressed and packaged.

Saturday arrived with much anticipation. Eloise and Thomas were very nervous for neither knew what to expect at the theater. They were both fearful of embarrassing their benefactors. Charlotte did everything to dispel their fear and acted like going to the theater was an everyday occurrence. Before the carriage arrived, everyone gathered in the parlor. Eloise was the last to arrive. When she entered the room, nobody spoke. Thomas walked forward and took her hands in his. "Eloise, you are the most beautiful creature God ever created," he said and kissed her hands.

The theater was a wonderful experience for Thomas and Eloise. After returning home, Eloise hugged Elrod and Charlotte, "You have been so kind and generous, how will we ever repay you?" The old couple held hands and smiled, "It is you to whom we owe a debt. Before you entered our lives, we were just two old people existing from day to day. You have brought life and cheerfulness to this house. Now we are eager for each new day. We have grown to love you both."

Chapter 36

From that time on, the relationship changed from one of employer and employee to a family. Thomas and Eloise ate their meals with the old ones when they were not dining out. Elrod and Charlotte began accepting invitations to social events and dinners they had declined for years. The four of them attended the theater, went to the circus and numerous sporting events.

Elrod and Charlotte were extremely generous with the young couple. Elrod offered Thomas a fine gold watch and chain. When Thomas declined, Elrod insisted saying, "I have several and you have none. It would be a favor to me if you would accept it." Thomas gratefully took the watch and shook his benefactor's hand.

One day Charlotte asked Eloise to accompany her to her room. Upon arrival, Charlotte beckoned Eloise to her closet where her jewelry was kept. Opening a drawer in the cabinet revealed many beautiful pieces of jewelry. There were rings, earrings, bracelets, necklaces, broaches and pins. You may have any of these bobbles you fancy. "I cannot," Eloise said, "they are very valuable, I cannot accept any of them."

"Posh," said Charlotte. "They are merely things, the true value in life is those you love. A beautiful girl deserves beautiful trinkets."

"I just cannot," replied Eloise in a choked voice. "Very well then, I shall decide for you." Charlotte selected a beautiful emerald ring with two diamonds and slipped it on Eloise's finger. "The green stone is perfect for you and goes well with your red hair," she smiled. Next, she placed a lovely bracelet on her wrist. She picked up an exquisite gold necklace and Eloise began to weep. "Enough, enough," she whispered. "You are too good to me."

"I have no one else to give things to love, and it would please me to see you wear jewelry I once wore."

Thomas and Eloise did not let this generosity go unrewarded. When Elrod's health began to deteriorate and he required more and more assistance, Thomas became his shadow, being there whenever Elrod needed him. Likewise, Eloise tended to Charlotte. Now doing all of the housework and almost all of the cooking for her, Charlotte was able to conserve her strength and spend time with Elrod. They would sit in the parlor holding hands, saying little, just enjoying being near each other.

One day Elrod asked Thomas to help him to the parlor and to fetch Eloise and Charlotte. When all four were assembled, the old ones on one couch and the younger on another facing, Elrod asked Thomas to pour them all a glass of brandy. When all had glass in hand Elrod began: "Charlotte and I are old, and my health is declining faster than I would prefer. I believe I shall depart this world in the very near future." At this point Eloise began weeping softly. Thomas choked up and his eyes teared.

Charlotte on the other hand, was clear-eyed and intensely alert. Elrod started to speak then faltered, and Charlotte immediately took over. "My dear Elrod was highly regarded and extremely successful in the banking industry. He made far more money than we needed and his wise investments made us quite wealthy. With no family of our own, we donated to those less fortunate. As we have both outlived everyone in our respective families, we had planned to leave what was left of our estate after the crown took most of it, to charity. Then you two entered our lives. Although you were initially hired as employees, we grew to love you and you became our family. Now we wish to make you a proposal. We would like to legally adopt the two of you. As our children, you would inherit the bulk of our life's work rather than the crown getting the lion's share. Lord knows the crown doesn't need our money for the royals are quite rich enough thank you. The inheritance would provide the both of you a fine lifestyle and you could carry on the philanthropic efforts of Elrod and myself. The income from the investments and properties alone will provide for you for the remainder of your lives and the lives of your children and grandchildren. Should you agree, our solicitor will want to meet with you as there is much paperwork to be done."

Thomas and Eloise looked at each other and Eloise spoke, "Although we already love you both and it would be a great honor, Thomas and I need to talk this over." Now composed, Elrod with a big grin said, "You best hurry, times running out, but before you go let us not allow this brandy to go to waste." Through this all, the brandy had been forgotten and everyone was holding full glasses. Everyone laughed and touched glasses. The brandy disappeared in a flash.

In her room Thomas and Eloise were silent. After some time had passed, Eloise spoke, "What shall we do Thomas, they are offering us a fortune and we have deceived them."

"Not intentionally," he replied, "we were hired as servants."

"Yes," she said, "but we became more than servants and we both benefitted from that."

"What do you propose we do?" he asked. "We must go down and tell them the truth."

"Then let us wait until after supper," he said.

Chapter 37

The dreaded moment arrived and everyone was seated in the parlor. "What have you decided?" asked Elrod. "We decided you must know the truth about us, so you may wish to withdraw your offer. Thomas is not my brother. We met on the streets when both of us were beggars. Thomas escaped from reform school and I escaped from the workhouse. We have no family save each other. Even though we love each other, Thomas and I have lived as brother and sister and have never done otherwise. We did not intend to deceive you or take advantage of you. We only needed work to survive. You both have been more than generous and we appreciate and love you both. We will leave immediately if you wish." Both Thomas and Eloise hung their heads. Both were ready to get up and leave.

Elrod looked at Charlotte, and neither had any expression. For the longest time they just stared at each other. Then Elrod showed a hint of a smile and Charlotte began to snicker. Then they both started laughing, laughing so hard they both had tears running down their cheeks. "We knew as much from the very beginning," Charlotte said through her laughter. "Elrod is a very suspicious character and did some checking up on the two of you before you arrived for supper that first day. He has contacts in very high places including a long friendship with the Chief Constable. It didn't take long for him to find out there was an inmate missing from the workhouse and another from the reform school. And you two just matched the description. After learning of the circumstances of your confinement, my dear husband paid your debt to the crown Eloise and he paid your fines at the reform school Thomas. He even settled your account over the incident of your stabbing a bloke, even though it seems the bugger deserved it. You are both free from your past. You were forced by circumstances to be petty thieves, but in your hearts, you are not thieves. Not once in the years you have lived in this house have you ever lifted a single item. The offer still stands, now we would appreciate your answer." Eloise began to cry. "Now, now dearie you mustn't cry," Charlotte admonished. "This is a happy time and we should all be happy."

"Assuming the offer had been accepted," Elrod said, "there is something on my mind I need to ask you two."

"Not now Elrod, it is really none of our business," Charlotte commented. "But it is love, and I must know before it is too late for me." Charlotte lowered her head and clasped her hands on her lap. Elrod took a deep breath and said, "Explain to me why have you not gotten married? It is easy to see you love each other, so what has prevented your marriage?"

"He has never asked me," Eloise responded with tears in her eyes. Everyone looked at Thomas. "I thought you would tell me when you were ready Eloise."

"You knuckle head Thomas, the man is supposed to propose to the woman."

"I, I," Thomas stammered. He looked at everyone, and then turned to Eloise, "Would you marry me?"

"No, no interjected Elrod, do it properly lad." Thomas was at a loss, for he knew not what the proper way was. Elrod got up and approached Eloise, "Stand here love," he instructed. "Now Thomas, you get before Eloise and go down on one knee. Now take her hands in yours, look her in the eye and ask her." Thomas did as he was told, and as he gazed up at Eloise his heart almost burst, for he loved her so much. "Say it boy, say it," Elrod laughingly said. Thomas took a deep breath, "Eloise, I love you more than life itself, and would be honored if you would consent to be my wife." Eloise weeping uncontrollably could only nod her head. "That's it son, now you've done it." Elrod clapped his hands and said, "I'll fetch the brandy, and we have cause to celebrate."

"We shall have a grand wedding at the Cathedral," Charlotte offered. "Please no," begged Eloise. "Let us have a quiet ceremony with just the four of us in attendance. You are our only family, and we would be uncomfortable surrounded by strangers at our wedding."

"So be it," voiced Elrod, "it shall be as you wish."

Chapter 38

And so, the planning began. Although the event would not be lavish, Charlotte insisted on Eloise wearing a wedding gown and Thomas decked out in a tuxedo. A couple of weeks later, they had obtained a license and the day arrived. The wedding took place in the office of a Magistrate who was a close friend of Elrod's, a simple yet solemn ceremony that left everyone in tears joined the two young lovers. After the wedding, upon returning home the bride and groom were surprised to find the house full of well wishers and a banquet laid out. Elrod had agreed to a simple ceremony but there was nothing said about an after the wedding party. And a party it was. There was champagne, fois gras, caviar, escargot, cheeses, cold meats, fresh breads, lobster, shrimp and crabs. There was a large table filled with gifts. As all in attendance were wealthy, the gifts were extravagant. "How can we accept all of this?" Eloise whispered to Thomas. "I fear we have no choice," he whispered back.

After all of the guests had departed and the family assembled in the parlor, Elrod started coughing, a racking cough that shook his whole body. His face turned bright red and his eyes opened wide. Thomas took off. "I'll collect the physician," he yelled as he raced out the door. Eloise and Charlotte helped Elrod to his bed and made him as comfortable as they could. His breathing was labored and he was sweating profusely. Eloise mopped his brow with a damp cloth while Charlotte held his hand and whispered, "I love you darling, please try to be calm."

Although it seemed an eternity, minutes later Thomas returned with the physician in tow. The doctor listened to the old fellow's heart and checked his pulse. He looked up at Charlotte and slowly shook his head. Charlotte leaned over Elrod and kissed his mouth. Elrod opened his eyes and spoke, “I know darling, I know, don’t fret, I am the happiest man on earth. I have a fantastic wife and two wonderful children, what more could a man want?”

Looking over at Thomas and Eloise, he said, “Take care of her for me.” Then he closed his eyes for the last time.

Chapter 39

The funeral was supposed to be small. With little family, Charlotte expected a short eulogy and a quick burial. What she hadn't counted on were the many, many people Elrod had done business with and how much they respected him. Then there were the myriad recipients of his generosity in attendance. Hundreds and hundreds of people marched behind the horse drawn hearse, including mothers carrying babies, and men who left their jobs when they discovered who was passing. "Hurrah, hurrah," they shouted, waving their hats and dancing along. Young boys and girls from toddlers to teens joined the procession. When the procession reached the church burial yard there was not enough room for everyone. Two gravediggers were standing by to fill the grave after the ceremony. One said to the other, "Must be a mighty important fellow in that casket." The other replied, "No, just a fellow who was loved by many."

Back at home after the funeral, the threesome sat in the parlor. Eloise wept and Thomas kept wiping his eyes. Only Charlotte seemed composed. She spoke, "Death is as much a part of life as living. Death is inevitable for all of us, so we should not be sad for the loss of someone special but jubilant for the honor of knowing them and having them in your life. Now we must get on with our lives and get Thomas adopted."

"Should we not wait a bit?" Eloise asked. "For what my dear? You know my wishes and those of Elrod, so why dilly dally?"

After a meeting with the solicitor and the signing of numerous documents, the adoption of Thomas went before the chief barrister. A few questions were asked of all parties, then the proceedings culminated with the barrister granting the petition. "Now that you are officially in the family, there are some things you must know about. Part of our estate is out of England. There is property in Australia, New Zealand, Ireland and Scotland. Although we have trusted employees that have faithfully served us for years, they too are growing old and with the passing of Elrod there is no one else to take charge after me, except you Thomas," Charlotte explained.

"I have no experience in managing anything," replied Thomas. "My education pretty much stopped when my sister Sarah left."

"I was unaware you had a sister, Thomas, this is quite a surprise."

"No, no Charlotte, Sarah is not really my sister," Thomas laughed. "Sarah is the girl who raised me in the orphanage. Sarah and me agreed we were brother and sister, that is all."

"That is a relief," said Charlotte, "that could have seriously complimented matters. Now I realize this will be a huge undertaking for you Thomas, therefore I have taken the liberty to enroll you in the college so you may be educated in business matters. You are an intelligent young fellow and will learn quickly, and I am competent to manage the business affairs while you study."

"As you were there to assist Elrod, I believe Eloise should attend college as well, so she can be of help to me," Thomas said. "That may be difficult," mused Charlotte. "It would be quite unusual for a woman to go to college. I learned the business by working with Elrod for all those years."

"Yes, you learned from Elrod, who in fact was your college. Eloise will not have that privilege."

"I see what you mean, Charlotte replied, "I shall contact the college dean forthwith. After all, we have made some sizeable donations to the college and I am sure he will be agreeable. This presents a bit of a dilemma, for if you are both attending college, that leaves me alone and I will surely need help." Thomas's face lit up. "Do you suppose we could find my sister Sarah in Dublin? She would be perfect."

"Well, we do have holdings in Ireland and we retain a solicitor in Dublin, so if she is still there, we shall find her. You realize that Sarah may have married and have her own family to care for. Or she may have moved on."

"Yes, that is certainly a possibility, but we should try," replied Thomas. "While you are in Ireland, there are several issues that must be addressed. Our solicitor recently posted a letter, which I have been too busy to sort out. We have a sheep ranch which has recently suffered some losses and the solicitor has expressed doubts that they are legitimate, so that will require some looking into. And you should visit some of our holdings to familiarize yourself with their working and meet the staff."

Chapter 40

So, it was decided. Thomas and Eloise would depart for Ireland within a fortnight. Charlotte would draft letters of introduction for Thomas and the young couple would set off to locate Sarah. "What a grand adventure this will be," cried Eloise. "We left Ireland indigent and in disgrace and will return successful and wealthy." The following week Thomas and Eloise set sail for Ireland. The trip across the Irish sea was uneventful, the weather was perfect and the seas were calm.

Upon arriving in Cobh, Thomas hired a motorcar and driver and they immediately set off for Dublin. Roads designed for horse drawn vehicles were most unkind to motorcar travel. By the time they arrived in Dublin, both Thomas and Eloise were sore, dusty, tired and hungry. Securing lodging was the first order of business. Not being familiar with the city, they stopped by the first pub they encountered. A pint of ale soothed their dusty throats. The lass serving the drinks recommended a house a short distance away that had rooms to let. Paying and releasing the motorcar and driver, they walked to the boarding house. The house was set back from the street, a cottage with a lovely yard and exceptionally well cared for. The mistress of the house was a woman who appeared to be in her fifties, wearing an apron over her dress and a bonnet on her head. She was a bit plump and short. Upon seeing Thomas and Eloise, she introduced herself as Mary McGuire. "Please come in dearies, you look like you have had a long journey."

"Aye, we have," replied Thomas, "and we are in need of a room and a hot bath."

"I've a fine room open, and it will suit you just grand. Please bring your bags and I shall fill the tub with hot water at once." Mary placed a huge kettle on the wood stove and began heating water. After both Thomas and Eloise had bathed and dressed in fresh clothes, they questioned Mary McGuire about the town. Thomas asked if she knew of a young lady fitting Sarah's description working as a nanny for a family with three children. "Gracious no," replied Mary, "I'd not be familiar with those of that class."

Next Thomas asked if Mary knew of the location of their solicitor. "Lordy no, I've never had the need for a solicitor and don't expect to ever meet one. You people of gentry would not be associating with the likes of me. "

"I assure you," said Thomas, "we began life in a far more humble station than where we are today. And we are most happy to know you, Mary McGuire." Mary lowered he head and said, "Thank you kind sir. Would you be inclined to eat here or would you rather dine in a fine restaurant?" asked Mary. "I'll wager you are as fine a cook as we shall find in the whole city," replied Eloise. Mary beamed, "I do make a rather delightful lamb stew," she replied. "Then lamb stew it is," said Thomas. The lamb stew was just grand, as was the soda bread and fresh churned butter. Thomas and Eloise ate until they were quite full. "We shall take a short walk while our food settles and then retire, for we have a busy day ahead of us tomorrow."

Chapter 41

The following morning after a fine Irish breakfast, Thomas and Eloise set out to locate their solicitor. Walking up and down the streets, familiarizing themselves with the city, Thomas and Eloise came upon a large crowd mulling about the front of a building. A young lad selling papers came by and Thomas asked what the excitement was about. "That's the court and they trying a woman for murder," he replied. "She went and pizened her master. Seems the old wanker had designs on her arse and she'd have none of it."

Suddenly the crowd erupted in a roar as a horse drawn police wagon pulled up. "The garda's here to haul her off to the prison," the newsboy yelled. The door to the courthouse opened and a group of people began pushing through the crowd. "Hang her," they yelled, "hang the murdering wench." Several officers were escorting a woman through the crowd. She was being punched and spat upon as she was navigated toward the street. People slapped at her and grabbed at her clothing. The woman had her head down and was sobbing, and her whole body was shaking.

Just as she was being put in the wagon, someone in the crowd grabbed her hair on the back of her head and pulled. Her head snapped up and she gave a moan. Thomas froze. "What is it Thomas?" asked Eloise. "That's Sarah, that's my Sarah," Thomas cried. "No, it cannot be," said Eloise. Thomas tried to get to Sarah but was grabbed by an officer. "What do you think you are doing?" he said as he roughly pushed Thomas back. "That's my sister, that's my sister Sarah," cried Thomas. "Well, your sister is a murdering bitch," said the officer. "No, it cannot be, let me go."

"You'll behave yourself or you'll be going with her," said the officer.

Eloise grabbed Thomas by the arm, "Come Thomas, we must know what has occurred before we can sort it out." Thomas reluctantly backed up and threw his arms around Eloise. Thomas sobbed, "Sarah is the kindest, gentlest person on earth, she would never harm anyone."

"Let's find your solicitor and see what he knows," said Eloise.

The letter of introduction Charlotte had given Thomas noted the solicitor's name was Sir Rodney Washburn of the firm Blankinship, Blankinship & Washburn. The letterhead noted the address was just a block distant. Hurrying to the office of B B & W, Thomas and Eloise entered and were addressed by the receptionist. "How may I help you?" she inquired. "We wish to see Sir Rodney Washburn," said Thomas. "Are you expected?"

"No, we just arrived in town." She replied, "I'm afraid Sir Rodney is rather busy though I will be happy to schedule you."

"That will not do, we must see Sir Rodney immediately," replied Thomas raising his voice. A gentleman stepped out of his office and asked, "Is there a problem?" The receptionist said, "This couple insists on seeing you Sir Rodney."

"I'm rather busy at the moment, please schedule." Thomas handed Sir Rodney his letter from Charlotte. He read the letter and looked up at Thomas. "It appears I work for you sir, please come into my office."

Sir Rodney was looking at his future. The firm's most important and valued client was sitting before him. "What may I help you with sir?"

"There was a young lady charged with murder in court today."

"Ah yes, I have been retained by the crown to prosecute the case. There is no doubt of her guilt and I intend to see she hangs."

"Then you must relinquish your role as prosecutor and defend this person with every tool at your disposal."

"But sir, the woman is guilty."

"She is not guilty! She is my sister and you will defend her or I shall retain another solicitor."

"It would be an embarrassment to the firm if I were to withdraw as prosecutor."

"I've no time to argue, my sister must be defended. You are discharged as my family's solicitor immediately. You will prepare our entire file to be collected tomorrow by our new solicitor. Good day sir." Thomas and Eloise left the building and retired to a nearby pub. "I must see my sister and sort out what happened."

"Thomas, you have not seen Sarah for many years and she may have changed."

"You do not know her as I do. Sarah raised me, she defended me and she sacrificed for me. She is incapable of harming anyone." Returning to the cottage, Thomas and Eloise planned their next move. "We must secure competent representation for Sarah. Tomorrow I shall find the finest solicitor in Ireland."

Chapter 42

The following morning after breakfast, Thomas and Eloise set out. Their inquiries directed them to several solicitors, but none which Thomas felt would help Sarah. Each wished to offer some sort of compromise. Strictly by chance, while taking a shortcut through an alley, thy came upon a sign which read, Alford P. Little, solicitor.

With nothing to lose they entered the office. There was no receptionist, there was no one at all. "Hallo, hallo, is anyone here?" Shortly there was an answer, "I'm coming, I'm coming, please be patient." A tiny woman appeared. "May I help you?" she inquired. "We would like to see Alford P. Little if you please."

"I am Alford P. Little," she responded. "But you are a woman," said Thomas. "Yes, my father wanted a boy so he didn't want to waste the name Alford. My middle name is Penelope. "But you are a solicitor are you not?"

"Yes, I practice before the bar, although I must confess, I have little business. No one wants a female solicitor, especially such a tiny one."

"Have you heard of the case against my sister for the murder of her master?"

"Everyone has heard of that case. The woman killed her master with poison for molesting her."

"She is innocent," replied Thomas. "She is my sister and I know she could never kill someone."

"Every person is capable of murder under the right circumstances," replied Ms. Little. "Not Sarah."

"Do you believe a person is innocent until proven guilty?" inquired Eloise. "I do," replied Alford P. Little. "Would you defend my sister?" asked Thomas. Ms. Little thought for several minutes then replied, "I would have to speak with her before I can answer that question."

The following morning, Thomas, Eloise and Alford P. Little arrived at the prison. They were ushered into a filthy room with only two chairs. After a few minutes a guard brought Sarah into the room. Sarah had on a flimsy dress and nothing else, not even shoes. She appeared to be in a daze and not cognizant of her surroundings. She looked at the people gathered as if they were not there. Thomas stepped forward, and in a low voice said, "Sarah, I am Thomas, your little brother." Saying nothing, Sarah looked at Thomas as though she had never seen him before.

Thomas began to sing a lullaby that Sarah sang to him every night to help him go to sleep. Slowly Sarah began to hum along with Thomas. She looked into his face, her eyes focused and she began to weep. "Are you truly my little brother?" she asked. "Aye, and I've come to help you." Sarah fell into Thomas's arms and sobbed. "What has happened my love, how are you in such a predicament?"

"I do not understand," she replied. "My employer died and I have been charged with his death." Alford P. Little spoke up, "Did the man molest you?"

"No, never. He was kind and always proper with me." The solicitor asked, "Who then said you were being molested?"

"His wife," replied Sarah. "Why would she say such a thing?" was the next question.

"I would often hear them arguing and shouting at one another," Sarah replied. "What were they arguing about?"

"Finances as best as I know. His business had taken a turn for the worst and they were having difficulties paying their bills. I would hear her accuse him of all sorts of nefarious activities. I no longer received my salary, but it didn't matter. I loved the children and enjoyed being part of the family. The missus changed after she suffered a miscarriage two years back. For a long time, she would not leave her room. She would not bathe or take care of herself. She ignored the children and her husband. Sometime later, she became angry. She cursed at everyone and several times she struck me. She accused me of plotting against her and trying to steal her husband. She said I was turning her children against her and she hated me."

Alford P. Little spoke up, "If Sarah is telling the truth, it would appear her mistress is the guilty party. She was driven mad by the loss of her child. In her deranged state of mind, she needed to blame someone for the tragedy. I believe her intentions were to poison Sarah and she mistakenly poisoned her husband."

"Can it be proven?" asked Thomas. "It will be most difficult," replied Alford P. Little. The magistrate is usually sympathetic toward a grieving widow."

"Will her children testify on your behalf?" she asked Sarah. "Oh my, I could not ask children to testify against their mother."

"Not even if your life depended on it?" Sarah replied, "No, I just couldn't."

Thomas spoke up, "I shall engage the services of an investigator. Perhaps he will be able to sort this out." Thomas asked the officer in charge of Sarah if he knew of anybody in that line of work. "Aye, there's a retired Captain who is for hire." Thomas wrote down the information. Bidding Sarah goodbye and assuring her they would do everything possible to prove her innocence, the trio left.

Chapter 43

They arrived at the office of retired garda Captain Seamus O'Flattery. Actually, his office was located in his home. The house was in a rather nice section of town surrounded by homes of similar construction. Entering through the iron gate, Thomas approached the door and dropped the knocker. A minute or so later the door was opened by a young lady. "May I help you?" she inquired. "We would appreciate an audience with Captain O'Flattery," Thomas replied. "My father is rather busy at the moment, would you like me to schedule an appointment?"

"Our needs are most urgent and a young girl's future is at stake. We have sufficient funds to compensate your father for his efforts." Thomas gave the young lady the letter of recommendation Charlotte had penned. She glanced at the letter, looked up at Thomas and said, "Please step inside, I shall show this to my father and return shortly." A few minutes later a gentleman approached Thomas with his hand outstretched. "I am so pleased to meet you sir," he said. "I am sorry for the loss of your father. I had some dealings with him a while ago before I retired. I must confess I did not know Sir Elrod had a son, much less a married one."

Thomas said, "Sir, we wish to retain your services in the interests of a very dear young woman who has been falsely charged with taking the life of her master."

"Is this in reference to the young woman accused of poisoning her master?"

"Quite so," replied Thomas. "I have known this person all of my life and consider her a sister. She is incapable of this crime and could never harm a fellow human being."

"Interesting, I understood the evidence bore out the charges."

"Not really," replied Thomas. "Her master was a grand fellow and their relationship was one of mutual respect. The wife is the accuser, who believed her husband and the young lady were more than employer and employee. The claim is absolutely false and you must prove her innocence."

Thomas held out a cheque for fifty pounds, saying, "Here is your retainer."

"My goodness man, that would finance several investigations."

"Nevertheless, please begin immediately. We are staying at the home of Mary McGuire. You may reach us there."

Thomas, Eloise and Ms. Little departed and proceeded to a nearby pub for lunch. Once seated and drinks ordered, Ms. Little said, "You were very generous with the Captain's fee. I should appreciate a bit of a retainer myself." Thomas laughed, "I'm so sorry Ms. Little, please forgive me, I'm afraid my mind wandered off." Thomas removed several notes from his pocket and handed them to the diminutive solicitor. "Goodness me," she uttered, "I've not been in possession of this much currency in a very long time. Thank you sir."

Chapter 44

For several days Thomas tended to the business accounts as instructed by Charlotte. Each evening Thomas, Eloise and Ms. Little visited Sarah at the prison. They took her fresh clothing and food, but most of all they took her hope. Thomas paid one of the jailers to keep a watch over Sarah.

The prison was run on fear, intimidation and bribery. Once it was noticed that Sarah had benefactors she became quite popular. The jailers all treated her better than the other inmates, hoping to be rewarded for their efforts. The other inmates did what they could to gain her favor. Sarah being the kind soul that she was, gave some of her clothes to others and shared her food, although she had been cautioned not to by the jailer who was paid to watch over her.

Captain O'Flattery contacted Thomas by messenger requesting a meeting. Arriving at his home, Thomas was ushered into his parlor. "There are several issues we must address," he said to Thomas. "First of all, the widow insists she caught Sarah and her husband in a compromising situation. She said Sarah killed her husband because he would not leave his wife for her. Secondly, the garda have already convicted Sarah and would lose face if they looked incompetent. Finally, the chief justice has publicly stated he will see Sarah hanged for murder."

"What shall we do?" asked Thomas. Well, the garda and the chief justice can be swayed with a monetary inducement. The widow is another matter. She appears to be mentally deranged and out of touch with reality. I do not know how we can reach her."

"Keep trying and in the meantime take care of the garda and the chief justice."

A messenger arrived at the Mary McGuire residence the following morning. "Captain O'Flattery requests an urgent meeting with Thomas and his solicitor." Thomas, Eloise and Ms. Little arrived at the investigator's residence at half eleven. "What have you found?" asked Thomas. "I found the apothecary where the strychnine was purchased."

"Who purchased it?" asked Ms. Little. "The widow herself," answered the Captain. "Is this sufficient to prove Sarah's innocence?" asked Eloise. "We shall see," said the Captain, "the magistrate will make that determination." Proceeding to the magistrate's office, they were told the magistrate was at lunch. "We shall wait," declared Thomas. "It could be a bit of time, for the magistrate does enjoy his vittles," replied the receptionist. "Where is the magistrate dinning?" asked the Captain. "At the Pigs Snout Pub," she replied. "I would caution you not to disturb the magistrate while he is eating," she said. Thomas turned toward the Captain and instructed him to collect the magistrate and bring him to his office. "We will wait for your return."

The Captain hurried to the Pigs Snout Pub and entering, he observed the magistrate sitting alone at a table. The magistrate had nearly consumed his meal of fowl and oysters when the Captain approached. "Dear sir, may I join you and order more ale?" The magistrate looked at his nearly empty glass and replied, "Please sit down, Captain." Two pints of ale were ordered. The magistrate looked at the Captain suspiciously. "What is your purpose Captain?"

Before he could reply, the ale arrived. "That will be six pence," said the waiter. "And the meal?" asked the Captain as he reached for his purse. "The honorable sir has an account," the waiter replied. "Nevertheless, what is the charge?"

"Three shillings six," replied the waiter. The Captain gave the waiter ten shillings and said, "Put the remainder on the magistrate's account." The magistrate smiled and inquired, "What is it you want in return for your generosity, Captain?"

"An urgent matter which requires you to return to your office immediately dear sir." Draining his glass of ale, the magistrate said, "Very well, I am quite finished with my meal and can enjoy my pipe at my office."

The Captain and the magistrate returned to a waiting Thomas, Eloise and Ms. Little. "Now what is so confounded important?" asked the magistrate. Ms. Little presented the evidence. "Well now, this sheds new light on the crime," said the magistrate. "Will you now release Sarah?" asked Thomas. "Not so fast," replied the magistrate. "There are certain legal procedures I must follow. These things take time." Thomas laid fifty pounds on the table. "How much time is required?" he asked. The magistrate looked at the money. He called his receptionist. When she appeared, the magistrate instructed her, "It seems there has been a serious miscarriage of justice, draw up release papers immediately for the gentleman's sister."

After receiving the document that would free Sarah, the group hurried to the prison. They were greeted by the warden. After reviewing the document, the warden said, "It seems to be in order and we should be able to release the inmate tomorrow or the following day."

"That will not do," replied Thomas, "please release her immediately."

"I'm sorry sir, we are short staffed and it would require my people to do extra work for one inmate."

"If we were to compensate yourself and your staff for the extra work, would that hurry things along?" asked Thomas. "That would depend on how generous you intend to be," replied the warden. "I will offer you ten pounds and one pound for each of your staff," said Thomas. 'Very well, I have a staff of twenty so that will be thirty pounds," said the warden. "Done," said Thomas, and he gave the warden thirty pounds. The warden left to collect Sarah. The Captain said to Thomas, "I would wager his staff consists of no more that six, and I doubt that any of them will see one pound. The warden is a scoundrel, however it is worth it to get this unfortunate incident brought to closure. Sarah has suffered enough."

Shortly Sarah was delivered. As they embraced, Thomas told her how much he loved her and that they would never be separated again. Sarah sobbed, "I thought you were gone forever." A couple of years ago I journeyed back to the orphanage to try to locate you. I met Mary Curley and she told me of helping you with food after you ran away. After that no one knew of you.

"Ah, I've a long story to tell you, but first let's get you cleaned up and have dinner." After a hot bath and being dressed in some of Eloise's clothes, the trio set out for dinner. During the meal Thomas filled in the time after Sarah left until the present time. Eloise smiled and said to Sarah, "It seems we both had to take care of Thomas." Eloise explained to Sarah the situation Charlotte would be in if they attended college at the same time. Sarah said, "Then it is sorted, I will be Charlotte's handmaiden."

"No, you will be part of our family," said Eloise.

Chapter 45

The following day after purchasing Sarah clothes, shoes, a bonnet and a portmanteau, they accompanied her to the ship and helped her aboard. Thomas gave her currency and cautioned her to keep it out of sight. "We will return in a fortnight dear sister," Thomas said as he kissed her goodbye. Sarah and Eloise hugged and kissed each other on their cheeks. We are now sisters as well," said Eloise.

Thomas and Eloise proceeded at once to the office of Alford P. Little. Upon entering Ms. Little said, "I'm just preparing tea, would you care to join me?"

"That would be grand," replied Thomas. Once tea was served, there was little conversation. Finally, Thomas spoke. "Ms. Little, we have several pressing matters which will require a great deal of effort and much travel. Do you believe you are capable of undertaking two very difficult assignments?" Ms. Little hesitated for several moments. Looking Thomas in the eye, she spoke. "Although I am small in stature, and a female to boot, I am an extremely competent solicitor. I am quite capable of any legal situation, perhaps more so than many of my male counterparts. However, if you feel I am not the solicitor for you, I may certainly recommend others you may prefer."

Thomas looked at Eloise. She had a smile on her face and slowly lowered her eyes as if to say 'It is your decision sir.' Thomas looked at Ms. Little for a long time, finally stating his needs. "Ms. Little, both Eloise and I want you to locate our respective mothers. The last time Eloise saw her mother was several years ago in the village of Kanturk, County Cork. As for my mum, I know nothing. I overheard one of the Sisters say I was sent to the orphanage and me mum was sent to the Magdalene Laundry."

"There is a Magdalene Laundry in or near every city with a hospital," interjected Ms. Little. "Do you know your mother's name and where she was from?"

"No, I know nothing about her," answered Thomas. "Let's assume your mother was sent to the laundry because of you sir." Thomas cried, "What? How can you say such a thing?"

"It is common for an unwed young woman who has had a child to be sent to the Magdalene. You entered the orphanage as an infant, therefore it is of the same time your mother would have been committed to the Magdalene. Do you recall in what town the orphanage was located sir?"

"Near Dingle," he replied. "Then that is where I shall begin to sort this out," Ms. Little said.

The following day Ms. Little departed to Dingle. Thomas and Eloise pondered their next move, which was to find her mum. They set out for Kanturk.

Arriving in Kanturk, Thomas and Eloise booked a room for two days. After a short rest they set out to explore the town. Having been so many years, the town had changed and Eloise had some problem finding her way about. After walking for the better part of an hour, Eloise began to recognize familiar streets and businesses.

Eloise stood at the corner by the butcher's then slowly turned about. "This way," she said to Thomas as she smartly started down the road. About a half kilometer later she stopped in front of a small cottage. The yard was overrun with weeds and the fence had many broken or missing boards. The cottage had been allowed to deteriorate. The thatched roof was bare in spots and the stoop was falling into ruin. "This was my home," Eloise softly told Thomas.

Shortly thereafter, the cottage door opened and a man stepped out. He was carrying a bottle of Paddy's Irish whisky and it appeared he had consumed quite a bit of it. Thomas spoke up, "Excuse me sir, is the lady of the house present?"

"There be no lady in this house," he replied. "What happened to the lady who lived here?" asked Eloise. "The old hag been gone several summers," he replied. "Did she die?" asked Eloise. "Nay, she just left one day." When Eloise asked, "Do you know where she went?" the man replied, "Who cares? She weren't worth nothing around here. Go on about yourselves. I ain't got time to answer your eejit questions."

Chapter 46

Returning to their room, Thomas attempted to console a heartbroken Eloise. "Do not fret my love, we will find your mother," Thomas vowed. "Let us go out and ask some questions," he said. As they stepped out of the door, a boy ran into Thomas and reached for his purse. Thomas grabbed the young ruffian by the arm and removed the purse from his hand. "You scoundrel, I should knock you about for stealing a man's purse."

"Lemme go you wanker," cried the boy. "Come now, that is no way for a young gentleman to talk," injected Eloise. "I isn't no gentleman, I's jus a poor cove who's hungry."

"Well, we can certainly remedy that," said Eloise. "Come Thomas, let us fill the lad's stomach." They proceeded to a nearby pub, where Thomas ordered a meat pie and a glass of ale for the boy. The boy did not hesitate and immediately attacked the pie the instant it was placed before him. "Gracious me, I have never seen a body devour a meat pie so quickly," said Eloise, as the boy drained the glass of ale. Thomas, remembering the many nights he went to bed hungry asked, "Would you like another?"

"I'd do it like I did the other," the boy replied. Another meat pie and another glass of ale were ordered. They both disappeared almost as rapidly as the first. The lad picked up a cigarette butt from the ashtray and lit it.

"Why you buy me food?" asked the boy. "We remember what being hungry is like, and wouldn't wish it on anybody," answered Thomas. "Bullocks, you people is rich, ain't never been hungry," said the boy. "We were very poor, as poor as you at one time," relied Eloise. "How'd you get rich?" he asked. "We worked very hard and were extremely fortunate," she answered. "Have you a name?" Thomas inquired. "Never had no given name, folks just call me Loser."

"What a horrid thing to call a person," Eloise cried. "Don't matter, I don't give a shite what people call me."

"Where do you live?" asked Eloise. "Wherever I wants," Loser responded. "Where are your parents?" she inquired. "Ain't got any," Loser replied. "What happened to them?" asked Thomas. "Not rightly sure, ain't never knowed 'em."

"Where were you brought up?" asked Eloise. "What's brought up?" he asked. "That means where you lived when you were a child," she answered. "I was in a workhouse until I run off," said Loser. "Where was that?" she asked. "Up north some place. Don't know no name of the place."

"So, Mr. Loser, how do you manage to take care of yourself? Where do you sleep and what do you eat?" The boy answered, "I sleep anywhere and I mostly eats what other folks don't want."

"When is your birthday?" asked Eloise. ""'Don't know, never had one," said Loser. "Do you know how old you are?" Loser replied, "Not sure about that either. How comes you people keep asking me all these fool questions?"

"Mr. Loser, we would like to help you. Would you like a job?" asked Thomas. "What kind of job?" he asked. "Doing different things, running errands and keeping your eyes and ears open," said Thomas. "I already hears and sees everything what's going on," replied Loser. "Well now, you must keep us informed as to what is going on," said Thomas. "You gonna give me money?" asked Loser. "Yes, how about a shilling a week?" said Thomas. "Hearing and seeing is two things, so it must be worth two shillings a week," answered Loser. Thomas began to laugh. "You are absolutely correct, two shillings a week. Here are your first week's wages," said Thomas as he handed Loser two shillings. "What I gotta do now?" asked Loser.

Thomas asked, "Do you know the cottage down that way?" as he pointed, "the one with the broken fence and the roof in need of repair?"

"Course I do, that's the brothers' place." Thomas replied, "The brothers? I do not understand."

"There's two brothers. They ran off the young miss, then they ran off the missus, then they kilt their pappy, and now they owns the place."

"They killed their father and they are not in prison? How is that?" asked Eloise. "Nobody ain't never found his body," Loser said. "What happened to the young miss?" asked Thomas. "She done disappeared years ago, never seen 'round here since," the boy replied. "And the missus, what about her?"

"After they turned her out, the old woman wandered about for a bit then she was gone," Loser told them. "Does anyone know where she went?" asked Eloise. "Nay, some say she lives up in the mountains."

"Will you look for her?" asked Eloise. "That's my job, to find someone who is lost?" asked Loser. "Yes, for she is my mother, Joyce Monahan," replied Eloise. "Here is a pound," said Thomas as he handed Loser the money. "It is for an emergency so do not waste it." Loser started off with high hopes. Thomas and Eloise retired to their room and were discussing the events of the day. A couple of hours later, a feeble knock interrupted their thoughts.

Opening the door, they found Loser, lying on the stoop. Thomas lifted Loser up on the bed. One eye was swollen shut, his lip was split, and he had several bruises on his face. Blood ran freely from his nose. Thomas called for a doctor. The doctor arrived and began administering to Loser. After cleaning his injuries and bandaging his wounds, the doctor said, "He has suffered several blows to the head, but he should recover fully in a few days."

Chapter 47

After two days, Loser was almost back to his previous self. Thomas asked what had befallen him. Loser said he was walking along playing with the money when he was attacked by the brothers. They beat him and took his money. Thomas was incensed. "Those scoundrels will pay for this!" Although Thomas was not a man prone to violence, his anger was certainly directed toward the brothers.

"Thomas dear, you must calm yourself," said Eloise. Thomas said, "You are right Eloise, let us find out if the brothers actually own the house that belonged to your mother. The tax collector will know who is listed as owner on the tax rolls," and they set off to locate his office. Upon finding him, they were informed that the owner of the house was Joyce Monahan. The deed was recorded in her name after the death of her husband. "Then how can those two wankers have possession?" asked Thomas. "Thomas dear, your language please," Eloise said softly. "My apologies love," said Thomas, "I'm just so upset."

The tax collector said the taxes were several years in arrears, but the property was so run down they didn't take possession of it. "Please give me something in writing to take to the Constable," Thomas said. After paying the back taxes, the tax collector penned a document showing the house was owned by Eloise's mother. Thomas and Eloise proceeded to the Constable's office and asked that the brothers be evicted immediately. Later that day, the Constable and a half dozen of his men went to the cottage and arrested both brothers on trespassing charges. "We shall take possession of my mother's cottage and make it proper for her return," said Eloise. Immediately they set out to locate a carpenter, roofer and grounds man. The local pubs provided the workers they needed. After giving each their instructions and money for materials, Thomas and

Eloise returned to their room.

"Your mother and father were respected member of this community," said Thomas. "Someone must know of your mother's whereabouts. We must begin asking around. You go to the local businesses and I shall check out the local pubs."

"Now Thomas dear, there are several pubs in this village. A pint in each and you will be wooly headed before you get to them all." Thomas laughed, "I will drink only a bit of each pint so as not to get wooly headed." Eloise answered, "I was but teasing you, my dear."

Eloise began with the butcher shop. Upon entering, Eloise observed a young fellow behind the counter. "May I please talk to the butcher?" she asked. "I is the butcher, whatsha thinks I be doing here iffen I isn't the butcher?"

"Oh dear, I am so sorry. The butcher I remember is much older."

"That be me da," answered the lad. "Is he available?" inquired Eloise. "Nay, he be taken a nap. If you wants some meat or fowl I get it for you."

"Actually, I would like to ask him some questions. I am looking for my mother, who I haven't seen for some while."

"Me da don't got your mother, just him and me.'

"No, No I don't mean to infer your father has my mother. She was turned out of her home by her husband and his sons and we do not know where she went. Her name is Joyce Monahan and she lived down that road," Eloise said as she pointed. "I knows who she is, her name's on our paper for owers."

"Owers?" asked Eloise. "They's ones what owes us money fur not paying on their account."

"How much does my mother owe?" The lad opened the store ledger, and locating the Monahan account replied, "One pound six shillings overdue," he answered. Eloise gave the lad two pounds. "That should cover any interest accumulated," she said. "Have you seen or heard of my mother?"

"I seed her 'bout last year," the man responded. "Where was she?" Eloise asked excitedly. "Her was walking up the road toward Abbeyfeale." Eloise thanked him and departed.

Thomas entered the Horse and Buggy Pub. Ordering a pint, he looked around at the customers. Seeing a table with several older gentlemen, he walked over and excused himself. "Pardon me sirs, would you mind answering a question or two?"

“What is it son?” asked one of the men. “My wife and I are trying to locate her mother, Joyce Monahan.”

“I knew the Monahans,” said one of the fellows. “When her husband died, Joyce married a scoundrel who eventually booted her out of her own home. Then he disappeared and his two sons took over. Joyce stayed around for quite some time then her mind began to wander and she became a different person. Started talking to herself and became withdrawn. Some of us tried to help her from time to time but she would have no part of it.”

“Have you seen her recently?” Thomas asked. “Not for a while. She just disappeared about a year ago, hasn’t been seen since.”

“Thank you for your time.” Thomas walked out of the pub and saw Eloise exiting the butcher shop. Crossing the street, Thomas met Eloise and asked, “Anything?”

“Seems she disappeared about a year ago,” Eloise responded. “That is what I learned.”

“The lad in the butcher shop says she was last seen walking the road to Abbyfeale Limerick County about a year ago. Assuming she hasn’t returned, then that is where we should look next.”

Assuring Loser that they would return and he was still in their employ, Thomas gave him some money and arranged for him to charge food and drink at the pub. “Now don’t get carried away Mr. Loser,” cautioned Eloise. “That account is for you and you alone.” Loser said not to worry, he would continue to carry out his assignments.

Chapter 48

The following morning Thomas and Eloise set out for Abbyfeale. Upon arrival and after renting a room, they proceeded to the local Constable's office. The Constable was up in his years and from the size of his girth had lived well. After introductions and explaining the reason for their visit, Eloise asked the Constable if he had any knowledge of her mother. "We did have a woman fitting that description in town a while back," he said. "She first showed up about a year ago and was in town for about four or five months before I asked her to move on."

"Why was that?" asked Thomas. "Several of the town's people complained about her. I caught her begging a couple of times and took her to Father Patrick."

Thomas and Eloise left and proceeded to the church. Upon entering they found Father Patrick, who inquired if they had come for confession. "No Father, we are not Catholic. We have come to ask you about my mother," said Eloise. "And who might be your mother?" the priest inquired. "Her name is Joyce Monahan. My mother has no home and the Constable said you may have fed her a time or two."

"Ah yes, I remember the lady. The poor creature was unfed and unwashed. She seemed somewhat confused and was unable to articulate the reason for her circumstances. When questioned, she would only say she was searching for her daughter."

Eloise began to weep. "Do you have any idea where she may have gone?" asked Thomas. "I'm afraid not, she didn't even know where she was going. I did hear some time ago that she was seen on the road north, so you might try Newcastle West."

Chapter 49

Late the following day, Thomas and Eloise arrived in Newcastle West. After renting a room at a local pub, they went downstairs and ordered dinner. While waiting for their meal they could hear people at a nearby table. "I say it's a shame something like that could happen in our town."

"Well, she doesn't belong here and should have gone back to where she came from."

"So now she deserved what happened, huh?"

"She belongs in the loony bin not in the hospital."

"Well perhaps she will move on after she gets out."

Thomas was curious and approached the other table and excused himself. "We couldn't help overhearing your discussion. Is the woman in question not a local person?"

"Nay, she wandered in a couple of months ago. Nobody knows her around here."

"What happened to her?" asked Thomas. "She was set upon by a bunch of hooligans who began to chuck stones at her. Before they were stopped, the old one was struck several times. They took her to the hospital, and then they'll be taking her to the poor house."

Their meal was delivered, but they were unable to eat. Thomas paid for the food and they left to locate the hospital. Arriving at the hospital, Eloise asked about the indigent woman. The Sister they spoke to told them the woman had numerous cuts and bruises. Although none of her injuries were very serious, her mental state was of question. Eloise asked to see the patient.

They were ushered to a large room with many beds. Led to a bed on the far end of the room, they saw a person covered with a dirty blanket.

Eloise gently pulled the blanket back to expose the sleeping woman. Her hair was filthy and matted with dried blood, her face was dirty and covered with bruises. Bed bugs had been feasting on her body and she was malnourished. To Eloise it was the most beautiful face in the world. "It's me Mum," she cried as she wrapped her arms around the woman.

Ever so slowly, the old lady awoke, frightened by the activity. She looked at the people standing by her bed and then stared at Eloise. "It's me, Eloise," she cried. The old woman looked up and replied, "Me daughter has the same name."

"I am your daughter, you are my mum." The old woman continued to look at Eloise. For several minutes nothing was said. The old woman reached and cupped Eloise's face in her hands. She began to weep and shake uncontrollably. "Is it true, is it true?"

"Yes Mama, I have found you. This is my husband, Thomas." The old woman raised her hand toward Thomas. He took her hand and kissed it, "Now you have a son, dear Mother."

Thomas hired a private nurse to look after Joyce until she was discharged. She was moved to a private room which had been thoroughly cleaned. The bed had new linens and there was a tub for bathing. Thomas had her meals delivered from a pub close by. Compared to the standard hospital fare of soup and bread, the pub food was a feast fit for royalty. With the attention given to her treatment and her diet, Joyce regained her strength and her mental awareness rapidly. In less than a fortnight she was released from the hospital. A different person walked out of the hospital than the one who was carried in. The cuts were healing, the bruises fading, her hair was properly coiffed. Wearing clothes of the upper class, she was met by a carriage with footmen waiting to carry her off.

The locals were dumbfounded. "Here we had a lady of society in our midst and didn't even know it."

Chapter 50

Arriving in Kanturk, they proceeded directly to Joyce's cottage. When the carriage pulled up in front of the cottage, both Joyce and Eloise began to weep. The cottage had been transformed. No longer were there weeds, no longer did the roof need repair, no longer was the porch falling. Along with the hired workers, several of the people who had known the Monahans in better times had pitched in to help renovate the cottage. While the men worked fixing, the women worked cleaning and decorating. With the additional help, the cottage was finished sooner than expected and just in time for Joyce to return to her home of many years. Although healed from the stones, Joyce had difficulty accepting her good fortune after the years of deprivation she suffered. Every day she would look at Eloise and ask, "Is it true, is it true?" And every day Eloise would answer, "Yes Mama, I have found you." And Joyce would reply, "And now I have a son."

After he had delivered the ladies to the cottage, Thomas went looking for Loser. He located him in the pub having a meat pie and a pint. Seeing Thomas, Loser became emotional and began to cry. Thomas sat down at the table. Loser wiped his face and nose with his sleeve. "I got them damn allergies what makes you eyes water," he said. "Finish your meal and I'll take you to your new employer Loser."

"You cutting me loose are ya?" he asked. "Not really, just transferring you to a different member of the family."

"I gonna work for your missus?"

"No, her mother," replied Thomas. "You done gone and found her?" asked Loser. "Aye, and she is waiting to meet you."

Arriving at the house, two of the men who had been working on the property motioned Thomas to step aside with them. Thomas told Loser to go inside while he spoke to the men. After Loser left, one of the men took his hat off and in a very soft voice said, "We found the brothers' father. "Where was he?" asked Thomas. "He was buried in the yard behind the house. We informed the Constable and the two sons were charged with his death. The brothers said their father had died of natural causes after being drunk for several days. When asked why they had neglected to report the death, they said they were afraid of being evicted from the house. The Constable said we will let the judge sort it out."

When loser met Joyce, he asked, "Is you rich too?" Before she could answer, Eloise spoke up, "She is family Loser, and family shares what they have with each other."

"What's my job?" inquired Loser. "You will live here with me," answered Joyce. "You will help around the house and run errands for me. In return you will receive room and board and a stipend."

"What's room and board and a stipend?" asked Loser. "As I said, you will have a room here with me. You will have your meals here, and you will receive payment for helping me. Now there are rules that come with the job."

"What are the rules?" asked Loser. "First you must always be truthful, you must keep yourself clean and your room tidy. No swearing and no smoking in this house, and you must attend school!"

"What I need school for?" asked Loser. "So, you will be able to provide for yourself and your family when you are an adult. Are these terms of employment agreeable?" asked Joyce. "I guess," replied Loser. "Very well, we will need to upgrade your wardrobe as soon as possible."

"What's a wardrobe?" asked Loser. "Your clothes," she answered. "I gets new clothes?"

"Yes," Joyce replied. "And shoes?" Again, the answer was yes. "How about a cap?"

"A new cap as well. We will go shopping once you have bathed and had your hair trimmed."

After the shopping trip Eloise, Joyce and Loser met Thomas at the pub. Loser had his new clothes and was sporting a fine new cap. The clothes seem to have changed Loser, as he was beginning to act like a dandy. "Now Loser, clothes do not make the man, the man makes the clothes," said Thomas. "I ain't never had no new clothes afore," Loser answered. "You will become accustomed to them," said Joyce, "just do not allow the clothes to change you."

"There is one more thing we should do before you move into my house," said Joyce. "I want you to be seen by a doctor," she told Loser. "Why? I ain't sick," he said. "Just a precaution so we'll know you are good and healthy, Loser."

After a meal of meat pies and ale, Thomas turned to Eloise and said, "I am going to the Post Office to see if there is any word from Ms. Little."

"Go along Thomas, we will be just fine," replied Eloise. At the Post Office Thomas found a letter from Ms. Little posted just three days prior. Hurrying to see what was enclosed, Thomas tore open the letter. "I have located the orphanage where you were an inmate," she wrote. "The priest who was in charge of the orphanage died several years ago. By most curious circumstances I must declare. Most of the Catholic Sisters have either retired, died or transferred. One Sister of very advanced age did recall Sarah and the child she raised. Although she did not know if the infant had been given a name before he arrived, she believes Sarah named the child Thomas without a surname. The child was believed to have come from the Convent in County Limerick. It is my intention to leave immediately for County Limerick."

Thomas hurried back to the pub. Excitedly, he informed them of his letter and his immediate departure for County Limerick to catch up with Ms. Little. "Shall I accompany you?" asked Eloise. "Perhaps you should remain here with your mother for the time being," he replied. "Very well," Eloise replied, "there is much for us to do here. I do wish to get Loser enrolled in school for he has much catching up to do." Loser interjected, "I ain't in no rush for that."

Thomas hurried to his room to pack his portmanteau, while Loser was taken to the doctor's office. Shortly thereafter, Thomas hired a coach and was on his way to Limerick County. Loser was in the process of receiving a physical. The doctor surmised from his physical development and his teeth that Loser was twelve or thirteen years old. Joyce said, "Loser, today we found out about your age. You can choose either twelve or thirteen, and we will just pick today's date as your birthday." Loser thought about it for a few moments and said, "I'll be thirteen and today is me birthday." Joyce said, "Wonderful, now we'll go home and have a birthday party."

Chapter 51

Thomas arrived in Limerick County two days later. He rented a room not far from the Convent and began looking for Ms. Little. Aware of the secrecy maintained by the Convent when they are paid for certain services, Thomas felt that Ms. Little could offer sound advice on how to proceed. Thomas visited the stage stop every day hoping to learn of Ms. Little's pending arrival.

Three more days passed before Thomas was informed of the arrival of a coach from the south. Hurrying to the station, Thomas found Ms. Little inquiring about a room. "So nice to see you again Ms. Little," Thomas said as he touched his hat. "I hope your long journey was pleasant."

"It was a bit uncomfortable at times I must admit," she said with a smile. "The driver seemed able to locate every hole in the road. Nevertheless, we are here and anxious to proceed with our investigation." After securing a room for Ms. Little, they went to a nearby pub for lunch. "Ms. Little, how do you envision our being able to extract information from anyone at the Convent?" With a wicked little smile on her face, she replied, "Money. The nuns can usually be bribed. Their life is rather mundane, without the comforts most of us enjoy."

"How do we first approach them?" asked Thomas. "We shall ask for an audience with the Sister Superior, she controls everything within the Convent.

After a good night's sleep and a fine breakfast of oysters, shirred eggs, toast and fruit, they took a coach to the Convent. After stating their intention of meeting with the Mother Superior, they were informed she was otherwise occupied and they could meet with one of the other nuns. Shortly thereafter, a nun approached them. Thomas was startled by the woman's terribly scarred face. "I am Sister Mary Margaret," she whispered, "what can I do for you?"

"Dear Sister, we are seeking information about a young girl who was brought here many years ago," Thomas explained. "I am not allowed to discuss matters of the Convent with outsiders," she politely replied. "We understand your position Sister, though I am the son of that young woman," said Thomas, "and I am trying to find my dear mother. After my mother gave me life, I was sent to an orphanage in Dingle and my mother was sent to a Magdalene Laundry. As there are so many scattered across Ireland, I was hoping to find out where she was sent." Sister Mary Margaret began to weep. "I remember your mother well," she whispered. "I administered to her during your birth. I have prayed for you both lo these many years."

"Do you know my mother's name?" Thomas asked. "Her name is Erin O'Donnell, and she was sent to the laundry in Cobh." Tears rolled down Thomas' cheeks as he became overcome with happiness. "How can I repay you for your kindness?" asked Thomas. "Help me to get a transfer closer to my family in Kilkenny."

He grasped Sister Mary Margaret's hand and kissed it. At that moment a loud voice spoke, "What is going on here, how dare you touch one of my Sisters?" An older nun who was quite obese strode up and addressed Thomas. "I am sorry Sister, I was overcome. This kind Sister just gave me a blessing which touched my heart."

"Well then, a generous contribution would be appreciated," said the Mother Superior. "The Convent does not operate on thanks alone."

"Would you have an amount in mind?" asked Thomas. "I should think twenty pounds would be very nice," she replied. "I would like to do something in addition, for all of you kind Sisters," Thomas said. "And what would that be?" she asked suspiciously. "I would like to show my appreciation by having a grand dinner for you all," answered Thomas. "I see," the Mother Superior mused. "Would tonight be agreeable?" asked Thomas. "Very well," replied the Mother Superior. Thomas and Ms. Little left the Convent and went to the pub to order dinner.

That evening the food began to arrive at the Convent. There were fowls, fish, oysters, puddings and bread. Also there were copious amounts of spirits, wine, ale and Irish whiskey. The Sister Superior was delighted and wasted no time praying. The blessing on the food was very short and to the point. All of the other nuns sipped wine while the Mother Superior drank Irish whiskey. Before the meal was finished, the Mother Superior was quite full and completely inebriated. Thomas began talking to her of a transfer of Sister Mary Margaret to Kilkenny. At first the Mother Superior just laughed, but then Thomas said it was worth two hundred pounds to him if the move took place. The Mother called her scribe and dictated the formal transfer. After receiving the money, the Mother Superior said, "Take her with you when you go, she never was wanted here." Thomas, Ms. Little and Sister Mary Margaret departed together. Thomas gave Sister Mary Margaret sufficient funds to help her get transportation to Kilkenny and some extra for her personal use. Thomas thanked her for her kindness to his mother and promised to visit her whenever possible.

Chapter 52

Thomas returned to Kanturk with the happy news of his mother's last known location. Loser was beaming when he told Thomas of his birthday. "I be thirteen years and I got a birthday!" Thomas congratulated him and said, "There is one more thing we need to discuss. My dear Eloise and I have agreed we would like to adopt you, Loser."

"What does that mean?" he asked. "Well, it means you would be our son and we would be your father and mother."

"And her?" he asked, pointing at Joyce. "She would be your grandmother. And you would have our name as well."

"What's that?" asked Loser. "Rooney," replied Thomas. "So, I be called Loser Rooney?" Loser inquired. "Well, we will think about the Loser part," Eloise laughed. "You will need a proper name for the legal papers if you agree to become part of our family."

"I ain't never knowed no other name," the lad replied. "Well, you can choose a name to your liking. Have you ever heard a name you really liked?"

"Never gave it any thinking," said Loser. "The first thing is do you want to be adopted? Having parents means you will no longer be a vagabond. You will have responsibilities to your parents and to yourself."

"What's a vagabond?" inquired Loser. "A vagabond is a person who wanders about without a home," Thomas answered. "I gotta tell you now if I wants to be this adopted?" asked Loser. "Not at all," said Eloise. "You take your time and decide. There must be many questions you will want answered."

"Should you choose not to be adopted, you will still be in our employ, and live with me as long as you wish," said Joyce. "Okay, I'll sort it out," said Loser.

Thomas took Eloise aside and said, "We must depart for Cobh. I must locate my mother." Eloise said, "We can leave as soon as I pack a few things and you hire a coach." Informing Joyce and Loser that they would be leaving at first light in the morning, Thomas hurried off to hire a coach.

Chapter 53

The journey took two days, and arriving in Cobh Thomas rented rooms in a hotel a short distance from the Magdalene Laundry. The laundry was a brick building in need of repair. The grounds were overgrown with weeds and most of the foliage was dead or dying. Eloise began to weep. "I cannot imagine living in such a horrid place," she whispered.

The following morning, Thomas and Eloise approached the laundry. The door off the street appeared never to have been used. The hinges were rusty and Thomas wondered if the door would actually open. Thomas raised the knocker and dropped it several times. After waiting several minutes, he applied the knocker to the door more vigorously. Again, several minutes passed before a nun came around from the side of the building and inquired what their business was. Thomas told the nun they had come to visit one of the inmates of the laundry. The nun said, "We do not allow visitors." Thomas told her, "I am willing to make a generous donation if you would make an exception this time." She responded, "I must talk to the Head Sister first." She left Thomas and Eloise standing and disappeared around the corner of the building.

After a seemingly endless wait, the nun reappeared and said, "Follow me." She led Thomas and Eloise around the corner and in a door on the side. Another nun was waiting once they entered. "I understand you wish to make a donation," she said. Thomas replied, "I will make a generous donation if we are permitted to visit one of your inmates." She asked, "And just which one?"

"Her name is Erin O'Donnell," said Thomas. "We have two Erins," the nun replied. "Are they both named O'Donnell?" asked Thomas. "We only use first names here," she said. "Do you not keep records when the person is admitted?" asked Eloise. The nun said, "I will bring both of them to you and let you decide." Several minutes later the nun brought two women. They both were dressed alike in a plain cotton dress and wore no shoes, their hair was a tangled mess, and aside from their arms, they were filthy. Both kept their heads bowed and said nothing. Eloise stepped forward and asked, "Is one of you Erin O'Donnell?" Neither spoke.

The nun said, "There you are, neither is the one you seek. Please make your donation and leave." Thomas stepped in front of the two women. In a soft voice he said, "I believe one of you is my mother." One of the women raised her head just enough to look at Thomas' face. Tears began rolling down her cheeks. In a halting voice she spoke, "I had a boy child." The nun said, "I told you not to talk, now you will be punished." Thomas wrapped his arms around the woman and asked, "Are you Erin O'Donnell?" The woman nodded her head and collapsed in Thomas' arms. "I have found you Mother. Now I will take you away from this wretched place."

"No! You will not," shouted the nun. "She was given to us for life. She belongs to us." Thomas informed her, "She is my mother and she belongs to no one but herself." The nun was furious. "You cannot take her!" she hissed. "I shall remove my mother from your clutches and there is no power on heaven or earth that can stop me," Thomas told the nun, "now let us talk of a donation." Realizing she had lost, the nun said, "She is one of our best workers and it will take two to replace her. Her absence will be costly. I will need at least two hundred pounds," said the nun. Thomas paid the ransom, took his mother's hand and led her to the door. "But she has no shoes," cried Eloise. Thomas looked at the first nun and said, "Give me your shoes." When the nun hesitated, Thomas handed her ten pounds. Quickly she removed her shoes and gave them to Erin. Once outside, they went directly to the clothing store. Thomas told Eloise, "Help her pick out whatever clothes she needs. I am going to go to the hotel and rent her a room." After securing a room for his mother, Thomas waited in a pub en route to the hotel for the ladies. After a couple of pints and two hours had passed, Thomas began to grow concerned.

Finally, Thomas observed a coach coming. The coach held Eloise, his mother and a great quantity of boxes. Thomas stepped outside and began walking alongside the coach. "I was becoming worried," he said. Eloise replied, "Shopping is not done in a hurry dear Thomas, and your mother had nothing to start with." Erin spoke up, "I'm afraid she was determined to buy out the store, my son." Eloise accompanied Erin to her room to help her with her toilet. Thomas waited in the hotel restaurant after ordering dinner.

The ladies arrived in all of their finery. Erin was in a state of melancholy, unable to process all that had taken place in just a few hours. She constantly looked at her new clothes, at Thomas and Eloise. "Is it true, is it true?" she whispered. "Yes mother, I have found you," Thomas told her. "And now I have a daughter too," she replied.

For three days Thomas and Eloise told of their journey from Irish orphans to English gentry. Erin told of her years of mistreatment at the laundry. Not only were the inmates constantly worked, they also provided perverse amusement for the nuns. None of the payment for laundry or donations enriched the lives of the inmates. Rarely were any acts of kindness shown the inmates of the laundry, rather they were treated as slaves. Eloise asked Erin if there was anything she wanted to do now that she was free. "There is," Erin said, "I would like to see my parents if they are still alive."

"Why would you care about them after what they did to you?" asked Thomas. "They are still my mother and father, and I love them," she replied. "I bear them no ill will and want them to meet their grandson."

"Very well, then we shall make every effort to locate them. I will contact Ms. Little and set her off to find them for us." Thomas posted a letter to Ms. Little telling her of his mother's request, and instructing her to proceed at her earliest convenience to the village near Galway. A fortnight later, a letter arrived from Ms. Little. Joyce had contacted her by post informing her that Loser had run off. Ms. Little said she would leave for the village near Galway very soon.

"Why would Loser do such a thing?" asked Eloise, "We have always treated him well." Erin explained, "Too much of a change in his life. I should know, it is overwhelming." We will sort that out later," said Thomas, "We must focus on finding my grandparents."

Chapter 54

For several days, they waited anxiously for news from Ms. Little. Erin was enjoying her new life and getting familiar with all she had missed for so many years. From time to time, Erin would look at Thomas and say, "Is it true, is it true?" And Thomas would answer again, "Yes Mother! I have found you."

Finally, a letter from Ms. Little arrived. It said she had found the O'Donnell's, and she gave their address. Upon inquiry, they were informed there was a stage leaving for Galway in two days. They went shopping for a portmanteau of sufficient size to hold Erin's new wardrobe. Two days hence they were bouncing along the highway to Galway. After a two-day journey, they arrived in Galway and secured rooms. Over dinner that evening they discussed their plans for the next morning. Erin was anxious to see her mother and had a feeling of trepidation toward seeing her father.

Morning came and they set out by coach. Upon arriving at the house, Erin began to weep. The yard was no longer neat and the bushes were no longer trimmed. The fence was in need of repair. Thomas knocked on the door; shortly the door opened and the woman said, "Yes, may I help you?" Erin looked at her mother as tears rolled down her cheeks. "Mother it is me, Erin." The old woman stared at her long-lost daughter. Slowly she put her hands on her daughter's face. "The Lord has answered my prayers," she said and embraced her daughter. "This is my son Thomas, your grandson and his wife Eloise," said Erin. Erin's mother hugged and kissed them both. "Who's there?" yelled a voice from inside the house. "Duff, we have visitors," she responded. "Who is it and what do they want?" he yelled.

Erin's mother led them through the house into a bedroom. There in the bed lay Duff O'Donnell. "He has suffered a stroke," she said. "He has difficulty walking and needs help eating and dressing." Duff O'Donnell looked at the strangers and demanded, "What do you want? Are you some of those Mormons here to save me?" Erin stepped closer to the bed. "Father, it is me, Erin. This is your grandson Thomas and his wife." Duff looked back and forth first at his daughter then at Thomas. "I have no daughter," he said. "Ah! but you do," smiled Erin. "You have a daughter who loves you and a grandson who would like to know you."

"But I sent you away," her father answered. "Yes, I remember," said Erin. "We both made mistakes, but if you can forgive me, I can certainly forgive you." Duff lay there speechless. "Please Duff," said his wife. Duff looked at his daughter and tears filled his eyes. "Can you really forgive my foolishness?" he asked his daughter. "Of course, Father. The past is the past, we are a family again." Father and daughter hugged and kissed each other while both cried.

It seemed after Duff had his stroke, he lost his job and they had fallen on hard times. Erin's mother took in sewing and did laundry, but the income was not enough to provide the treatment Duff needed, or to keep pace with their expenses. They had been notified that they would be committed to the poor house if their situation did not improve very soon.

Erin decided she would stay with her parents and help her mother take care of Duff. Thomas enlisted the services of a nurse to assist whenever needed. Thomas purchased a wheelchair so Duff could get out of bed. He paid all of the O'Donnell's creditors and had the house, yard and fence repaired. He established credit at the pub and stores in town, having the bills sent to Ms. Little for payment. After a week of catching up, with a lot of crying, hugging and kissing, Thomas and Eloise said they must leave and sort out the problem with Loser.

Chapter 55

The journey back to Kanturk took three days. Arriving at her mother's house, they inquired about Loser. "He just disappeared," said Joyce. "Have you contacted the Constable?" Thomas asked. "Yes, that as the first thing I did," she answered.

Thomas went around town asking if anyone had seen Loser or knew of his whereabouts. With no success, Thomas went to a pub for lunch. There were many people in the pub and Thomas asked the bartender to ask for quiet as he wished to make an announcement. The bartender banged on the counter until all was quiet. Thomas addressed the crowd. "I am looking for a young lad of thirteen who goes by the name of Loser." Several in the crowd snickered. Thomas described Loser. A man in the corner stood up, "I seen a young fellow who looked like that when I was coming down from Newmarket this morning. He were walking along the road." Thomas thanked the man and went directly to the stables and rented a horse.

Arriving in Newmarket, Thomas saw a crowd gathering. "What is going on?" he asked a passerby. "The Constable is going to flog a young fellow for stealing," the man replied. "What did he steal?" asked Thomas. "A pie," was the answer. "A pie?" repeated Thomas. "Ay, the widow O'Keefe put the pie in the winder to cool and it disappeared. When she ran outside, she seen this rascal runnin' off," the man explained. "And did they catch him with the pie?" Thomas asked. "Nay, but the widow was sure it was him." Thomas asked, "Then where is the pie?" He answered, "Musta hid it somewhere I suppose."

Thomas worked his way to the front of the crowd just in time to see the Constable hauling Loser by the collar of his shirt. "A moment sir," Thomas intervened. "Are you positive this is the lad who took the pie?"

The Constable responded, “The widow said he was the one.”

“But did she see him take the pie?” Thomas asked. “No, but he was right there,” he answered. “What kind of a pie was it?” inquired Thomas. “It was a blackberry pie,” the widow O’Keefe shouted. “Look at this lad, does he have any evidence of blackberries on his face or hands?” Just then a commotion at the back of the crowd turned everyone’s heads. The crowd parted and a fellow dragging two lads by their collars brought them to the Constable. Both had blackberry juice around their mouths and on their hands. “I found these two behind that building eating pie,” he said pointing toward a shed. “Seems you have the wrong fellow Constable,” said Thomas. “Appears so,” replied the Constable. “You may go lad,” he said, as he released his hold on Loser.

Thomas took Loser to where his horse was tied. “Why did you leave, Loser?” He replied, “I don’t belong with no rich people. I’s a poor one who would embarrass you folks who done been so kind to me.”

“No Loser, we are very fond of you, and would like you to stay with us. However, if you wish to leave, I will not stand in your way. Should you decide to leave, I would like to give you some money to help you on your journey.” As tears ran down Loser’s face, he embraced Thomas and began sobbing. “I ain’t never had nobody be good to me as you been,” he proclaimed. “Let’s go home and sort this out Loser. You may always leave should you want.” So Thomas and Loser rode double on the horse back to Kanturk.

The following morning after breakfast, Thomas and Eloise began packing. Loser asked, “Where is you goin’?” Thomas told him, “We have some business to take care of, then we must return to England and begin college, so we will be prepared to help Charlotte with her businesses.”

“What’s college?” asked Loser. “It is a school,” replied Thomas. “You goin’ to school, but you is all growed up,” Loser observed. “There are many things we do not know and must go to college to learn,” answered Eloise. “Just as you should go to school Loser, so you will be better prepared to assume the responsibilities you will face in the future,” interjected Thomas.

“We must know Loser, if you intend to remain here with Joyce. For if you decide to leave, we must find someone to be here with her in our absence. However, if you decide to stay, you must do as Joyce instructs and you must go to school.” Loser looked at Joyce, then at Thomas and

Eloise. "I think I wants to be adopted, like you said."

"Wonderful," said Eloise as she embraced Loser. "We will contact Ms. Little and have her begin the required paperwork by the next post," Thomas said. It will take some time for the legal process to evolve and we will return when a court date is announced.

Everyone took turns hugging Loser while shedding tears of happiness. Then Joyce announced, "This calls for a celebration!" Eloise penned a list of what they needed and gave it to Loser with money for the purchases.

Chapter 56

"Loser has been away for far too long. What could be delaying him?" asked Joyce. Thomas said, "I'll go and see if Loser could use some help." Thomas went straight away to the butcher shop. "Has a young fellow been in to purchase some meats in the past few minutes?" he asked. The butcher replied, "No lad has been in this morning, sir."

Thomas proceeded to the pub. Upon entering he went and asked the cailin wiping the bar, "Has a young lad been in this morning to purchase some food and drink?"

"Why yes, a lad did come in. However, before he could place an order, he was pinched by two fellows."

"Did they say why they did this?" asked Thomas. "No but they must have been Garda Siochana, for they told him he was being arrested."

"Did they say why they were taking him?" asked Thomas. "No, they said not a word more."

Thomas went quickly outside and looked up and down the street for Loser. Seeing no one, he went to the stables. Finding the stable hand in the back grooming horses, Thomas asked if any strangers had been in this morning. The stable hand replied, "Yes, two came in a buggy this morning and left later with a small fellow with them."

"Which was did they go?" he asked. "East toward Mallow," he said as he pointed toward the road. "How long ago?" Thomas asked. "Within the hour," the stable hand answered. "They were in a hurry, paid me to groom and grain their horse and have it hitched and ready. They returned with the young fellow in tow and departed."

Thomas hurried back to the house and relayed what had transpired with Loser. "What shall we do?" cried Eloise. "We are scheduled to depart for England in two days and I am unable to pursue this at this time," said Thomas. "I will contact Ms. Little and have her retain Captain O'Flattery to bring Loser home."

Immediately, Thomas penned a letter to Ms. Little in which he relayed what had happened to Loser and instructions on hiring the captain to pursue the matter and sort it out.

Sadness prevailed in the house as concern over Loser was on everyone's mind.

Chapter 57

The following two days passed ever so slowly as Thomas and Eloise prepared for their return journey. After saying a tearful goodbye to Joyce, Eloise and Thomas boarded the stage that would carry them to Limerick, which was their first night layover. The day was cloudy and cool as they rode through the countryside passing through three small villages. Little was spoken, both being deep in thought. Finally Eloise spoke, "Thomas dear, since Loser came into our lives it has been like having a little brother. I don't know what I shall do if we are unable to find and recover him."

"Fret not my love, we will have Loser back before you know it," Thomas replied. "Oh Thomas, I am so worried," Eloise said softly. "We must remain positive, and expect all will be sorted out in due time," Thomas replied.

The stage arrived in Limerick just before nightfall. Thomas and Eloise secured a room in the hotel. After washing and changing clothes, they went down to dinner.

"I'm not really hungry," said Eloise. 'Nor am I," Thomas answered. "Though we must eat, for the journey tomorrow will be much longer. First though, I intend to have a glass of Paddy to wash the road dust from my throat."

"In that case I would enjoy a bit of white wine," replied Eloise. "Perhaps a little libation will lift our spirits and encourage our appetites," she added.

After enjoying their refreshments and the warmth of a peat fire, Thomas said, "Now that I am relaxed my appetite seems to have returned. Shall we order my dear?" he asked. "Yes, please order fish and a salad for me."

“I shall enjoy a meal of bangers and mash, and a pint of Guinness,” said Thomas. The meal was delivered and in typical Irish fashion looked and smelled delicious.

Although they ate in silence, Loser was on both of their minds. Thomas could not understand why Loser was arrested.

Returning to their room and going to bed, they both fell asleep almost immediately. It had been an uncomfortable day with the long coach ride and concern over Loser.

Chapter 58

After a breakfast of tea and biscuits the next morning, Thomas and Eloise boarded the stage for the next leg of their journey. They took with them a lunch of sausages, soda bread and cheese.

They traveled through Nenagh and Roscrea on their way to the next layover at Portlaoise. Unlike the previous day, the weather had changed overnight, growing windy, cold and rainy. Mud hampered their progress as the horses lost purchase on the road and tended to slip and slide. The stage driver had no choice but to slow down and walk the horses. Eloise exclaimed, "It is fortuitous that the Inn insisted we carry a bit of lunch for we will surely arrive too late for dinner." Expecting to arrive at Portlaoise shortly after sunset, they finally reached their destination about midnight.

With only a few hours of fitful sleep they boarded the stage once more. Thomas spoke up, "I just accepted that the motorcar is superior and will replace the horse and stage."

"Why is that dear?" asked Eloise. "Well for one, the motorcar does not get tired and need resting. Secondly, the motorcar runs on petrol and can go for prolonged periods without refueling. The motorcar does not bolt or rear up. And finally, the motorcar is far more comfortable than a stage or buggy. It is my understanding that in America everyone drives an automobile. Hardly anyone still uses horses and mules."

"If you say so my dear," said Eloise with a smile.

Stopping at Kildare for lunch and to exchange horses, they began the final and rather uneventful leg of their journey to Dublin. The weather had cleared and they were able to pull back the covers on the windows for some fresh air. Arriving in Dublin, they proceeded to the ferry terminal. The next ferry to Liverpool would leave in the morning at 7:00 am.

They purchasing their tickets to Liverpool and then rented a room. After washing and changing clothes, they proceeded downtown to the Temple Bar Pub. Famous for its "pub grub" the Temple Bar was the most popular pub in Dublin. Thomas ordered Galway Bay oysters and a steak. Eloise ordered lamb stew.

While waiting for their dinner, Thomas enjoyed a glass of Paddy's Irish whisky and Eloise sipped on an Irish Lady cocktail. "My goodness Thomas, I do feel a bit wooly headed," exclaimed Eloise after a couple of sips. "It's the excitement of the day, my love," Thomas laughed. "I think not," she replied. "No more until I have eaten my dinner."

The Galway Bay oysters arrived first and always the gentleman, Thomas offered Eloise the platter. "No thank you Thomas. Raw oysters right now would not be a good idea." Their dinner arrived and Thomas wasted no time devouring the rare steak while Eloise slowly began to eat. "This is so good I feel better already," she exclaimed. After finishing their dinner, Thomas and Eloise strolled through the various shops and ended up at their rented room. "A good night's sleep will do us both good," said Thomas.

Eloise hesitantly spoke. "Before we retire, there is something I must tell you Thomas."

"What is it, Eloise?"

"We are going to become parents," she answered.

"I know, once we adopt Loser we will officially become parents, right?"

"No love, I mean you are going to become a da and me a mum." Thomas looked at Eloise with a shocked expression. "Do you mean?"

"Yes love, I am with child."

"There is no doubt, Mo Anam Cara (my soul mate)?"

"No doubt, Thomas. Are you upset?"

"No, a bit in shock perhaps, but certainly not upset." A few moments of silence passed, then Thomas embraced Eloise and tenderly kissed her. "I am now the happiest man in the whole of Ireland. All of my life I have thought about having a family. Unlike the way I grew up, but a real family. We will be the best parents in the world." Thomas wrapped his arms around Eloise and lifted her off the floor. Spinning around and laughing, the couple finally collapsed on the bed.

Chapter 59

Unable to sleep, Thomas and Eloise spend most of the night talking about their future child, and discussing various names for a girl or boy.

"I like Coleen for a girl," said Thomas.

"And what for a boy?" asked Eloise.

"Aidan, I think," he responded. "And what are your thoughts, my dear?" he asked.

"I think Connor for a boy and I'm rather fond of Aisling if we have a daughter," she answered.

"Well, we have plenty of time to sort names out. Now we must get some sleep for it will soon be morning."

The couple awoke at daybreak with the same giddy feeling they shared the night before. Over breakfast the couple would look at one another and break out laughing. They had a secret from the whole world, a secret theirs and theirs alone. "Do you know when the child will come?" asked Thomas. 'I'm about three months in," she replied. "I had to inform you, for soon it will become apparent as my stomach will certainly give me away."

"I look forward to informing Charlotte that she is to become a maimeo (grandmother)," offered Eloise. "As she never had children, she never could expect to be a grandmother. She will be so excited, I'm afraid our child will be spoiled rotten long before it arrives."

"We slept a bit late and must leave right away Thomas," Eloise said. "I'm almost ready. I'll ring for the porter to carry our portmanteau to the dock," he replied.

Arriving at the point of departure, they were hurried aboard the ferry. "If we do not cast off very soon, we may have to remain in port, for the weather is expected to turn for the worst," the mate told them.

"Are you positive it will be safe to cross?" asked Eloise.

"The storm is coming from the west and if we depart immediately, we should be safely ahead of the foul weather," replied the mate.

Chapter 60

Once aboard and after locating their cabin, Thomas and Eloise were happily discussing plans for their unborn child. Names were suggested back and forth until they both became confused over all of them. "There are many things we must purchase before our child arrives," said Eloise. "Although we have months to accumulate what our child will require, we must at least be aware of its needs. A bassinette to start with, then an infant bed, then a stroller, clothes and there is so much more," she offered.

"How do you know so much about babies?" Thomas asked. "Once I thought I might be with child, so I did some research," she admitted. "We should also look into a nanny for the infant, for we will both be in business school during the day."

"My sister Sarah would be perfect, for she raised me," Thomas said enthusiastically. "Thomas dear, Sarah will be occupied in the service of Charlotte. The additional responsibility could very well overwhelm her."

"Well, let's see what Charlotte and Sarah think before we make a final decision," said Thomas.

Without warning, the boat lunged violently to the starboard side, then back just as violently to the port side. Both Thomas and Eloise were tossed to the deck of their cabin. Thomas helped Eloise to a sitting position and asked if she were injured. "No, I'm fine. However I am as frightened as I can be."

"I'll go topside and see what I can find out," said Thomas. The ferry was pitching from side to side and up and down over swells. The sea was becoming very rough and water was coming over the foredeck. Thomas encountered a deckhand and inquired as to the seriousness of the situation. "I've never seen the sea get so angry so quickly," the mate answered.

"Will we turn back?" asked Thomas. "Nay, we have already passed the halfway point and must carry on," he replied. "How much longer to Liverpool?" asked Thomas. "Normally about three hours, but in this weather most likely closer to five hours," the mate answered.

Thomas returned to the cabin and informed Eloise of their predicament. "There is nothing we can do except pray for deliverance and have faith then," offered Eloise.

The young couple tried to be cheerful as they discussed the adventures lying ahead. There was their child of course, the reunion with Charlotte and Sarah, the continuance of their education and the search for Loser.

Suddenly the ferry gave a tremendous lurch forward, then nosed down and the fantail lifted above the water. The screws were spinning crazily in the air. Just as quickly the bow of the boat rose up and the fantail smacked the water. The whole ferry began shaking. Eloise was thrown into Thomas, who clutched her desperately. The ferry rolled to one side, almost tipping over, then back to the other side. Objects in the room flew off their shelves and furniture tipped over.

Water began to drip into the cabin. "Are we sinking?" a frightened Eloise asked. "I do not believe so, at least I certainly hope not," Thomas answered. As the boat continued to vibrate and shake, the frightened couple could only hold each other and try to keep from being tossed about the cabin.

Just as suddenly as it began, the boat seemed to slow down and the vibrations lessened. "I will go topside and see what I can learn," Thomas said. "Please do not leave me," begged Eloise. "It will only be for a minute, my dear. I must know what is going on."

"Promise you will hurry," asked Eloise. "I will be back before you know I'm gone," he replied. Thomas went up to the main deck to find it littered with all sorts of objects. The storm had torn stanchions from their mountings and numerous items lay broken on the deck.

Thomas located a crew member and asked if the boat was in any danger. "Not a bit," was the reply. "We had a ferocious squall hit us, but other than some minor damage we are just fine. The funny thing," he added, "was the fury of the storm pushed the boat forward and we will arrive in Liverpool sooner than expected."

Thomas hurried back to the cabin to give Eloise the good news. Thomas found her straightening up the cabin. "That isn't necessary my love."

"I cannot tolerate messes," Eloise replied. "Very well, I'll give you a hand. It will make the time go faster and before you know it, we will be back in Liverpool."

Chapter 61

The ferry docked shortly thereafter. As soon as their boxes and portmanteau were loaded on a carriage, they proceeded to Charlotte's home. Upon arriving, they were greeted by an overwhelmed Sarah. The three of them exchanged hugs and kisses and all shed a few tears. "Charlotte shall be so surprised," Sarah said.

Upon entering the home, Thomas inquired as to where Charlotte was. "In the drawing room," answered Sarah. "Her hearing is no longer as keen as it was and she probably did not hear your arrival."

As they entered the drawing room, they saw Charlotte sitting by the window reading a book. "Look who we have here, Missus," Sarah voiced. Slowly Charlotte turned around, and when she saw Thomas and Eloise she sprang from her chair and embraced them. "That's the fastest I've seen her move in some time," Sarah chuckled.

"Quickly Sarah, some brandy. We must celebrate."

"Yes, Ma'am," Sarah answered as she gave a slight curtesy. "And bring a glass for yourself," Charlotte added. Eloise spoke up, "No brandy for me if you please."

"Perhaps a glass of wine, my dear," offered Charlotte. "No, but I would enjoy a cup of tea," she said. "Is there anything wrong, my dear?" asked Charlotte. "No," Eloise replied, as a large grin crossed her face.

Eloise looked at Thomas and they both began to laugh. Sarah and Charlotte looked confused, and Sarah asked, "What is going on my brother?" Eloise took Charlotte's hands in hers, looked her in the eyes and said, "You are going to become a maimeo, dear Mother." For a moment Charlotte said nothing, then the reality of Eloise's words hit home. "Me a grandmother, the lord has certainly blessed me this day.

If only Elrod were here, he would be overjoyed."

Thomas looked over at Sarah and said, "You my dear sister, are to become an aunt." Sarah embraced Thomas, then Eloise. "Thank you both for this great honor."

Charlotte spoke, "I have enjoyed Sarah as my handmaiden and she has performed admirably, however this changes the situation."

"How do you mean, dear Mother?" asked Thomas. "Well, the way I see it, if you and Eloise are my children, and Sarah is your sister and will be aunt to my grandchild, then she is no longer my handmaiden because she is now even more like family."

"But Ma'am, I am not really Thomas's sister," Sarah protested. "You are his sister in every way but through blood. Therefore, you are family." Sarah clapped and hugged everyone while all shed a few more tears.

"There is one family member we are yet missing," said Thomas. "We must find Loser."

"While you were in Ireland, I had a telephone installed," said Charlotte. "Now you can communicate with your attorney in Ireland if she has access to a telephone."

"I will write her and see if there has been any progress in locating Loser, and send her your telephone number in case she can find a telephone."

"They are quite handy," Sarah spoke up. "We can order groceries by telephone and have them delivered."

"What is this world coming to?" asked Thomas.

The following week, the telephone rang. When Sarah answered, the operator said Solicitor Little was on the line for Thomas Rooney. Sarah showed Thomas how to use the telephone and he yelled "HELLO" as if he were shouting all the way to Ireland. "Just talk in your normal voice," Sarah instructed Thomas.

"What intelligence do you have for me, Ms. Little?" he asked. Answering she said, "Captain O' Flattery located Mr. Loser en route to a poor house near Ardee in Louth County. The Captain accompanied the officers and Mr. Loser to the poor house, where he was able to secure his release by paying his parents' debt. I believe Mr. Loser is on his way back to Kanturk and Ms. Monahan's home as we speak."

"Fantastic information," Thomas replied. Thank you for an excellent outcome, Ms. Little." Now that the situation with Loser was resolved, they would need to turn their attention to the immediate needs of Charlotte's business endeavors.

Sarah asked Thomas if they could take a walk, as there was an issue they needed to sort out. They told Eloise they would return shortly and stepped out into the morning air. "What is on your mind, my sister?" Thomas inquired. "I must make you aware of Charlotte's condition," she replied. "Her condition? I don't understand. She appears fine to me."

Sarah explained, "Charlotte fell down while shopping a fortnight ago. Although she seemed fine when she fell, she cracked her head and has been experiencing severe headaches."

"What do the doctors say?" a concerned Thomas asked. "The doctor is fearful the headaches will not only continue, but worsen. The doctor would like Charlotte to be hospitalized. A period of observation could determine if there is bleeding, which is putting pressure on her brain causing the headaches. The doctor called it a subdural hematoma."

"Then what?" Thomas asked.

"If it is a subdural hematoma, the doctor would operate to relieve the pressure. If that procedure was successful, Charlotte would be back to normal. If it is not pressure causing her headaches, the doctors fear it could be brain damage from the fall. That being the case, Charlotte would be prone to light headedness, and the probability of another fall is a real possibility. Brain damage would be inoperable. Oftentimes, that sort of injury heals itself in time. If not, Charlotte would be prescribed medication. The down side of the medication is the medicine carries with it the likelihood of dependence, meaning once she starts, she may never be able to go without it. In addition, stronger and stronger doses will be required as her body adjusts to it. One other thing, Thomas. Charlotte's condition requires a full-time nurse. Someone trained to recognize subtle changes in her cognitive ability, change of habits or temperament."

Returning home, Thomas found Eloise and informed her of Charlotte's condition. Eloise began to weep. "The sweet auld dear, I'm so sad for her."

"As am I," said Thomas. "She will need all of our love and support to get through this ordeal."

At the dinner table there was little conversation. Everyone kept glancing at Charlotte. Suddenly Charlotte grabbed her head with both hands. She closed her eyes and emitted a soft cry. After a few moments she looked up and smiled. "That was a rather good one," she offered.

"It is time we discuss your condition, dear Mother," Eloise said.

"I understand what the doctor has told me and what he has recommended, though I am quite frightened about going to the hospital. Over the years I have known numerous people who became inmates of a hospital and never returned home."

"Your condition is entirely different," spoke Sarah. "The doctor said if it is a subdural hematoma, the operation has been performed hundreds of times with extremely high success."

"Perhaps so. I am still frightened," whispered Charlotte.

"We intend to have a nurse brought in to care for you," said Thomas. "Not necessary," responded Charlotte. "I have decided to acquiesce to the doctor's recommendation and will enter the hospital the day after tomorrow. I have instructed my barrister to meet with us in the morning at noon. There are business matters and some minor changes in my will that must be attended to."

Chapter 62

The following morning the barrister arrived. After tea was served, the business began. Mostly Charlotte wished to be assured that her instructions regarding Thomas and Eloise were carried out. In addition, she included Sarah in her will. "Now in the possibility that I do not survive, everything has been sorted out to my satisfaction."

Two days later, Charlotte was committed to the Aintree University Hospital. Thomas, Eloise and Sarah visited Charlotte every day. Her spirits were high and she seemed to have accepted whatever fate had planned for her.

After one week the doctor informed her family that Charlotte did indeed have a subdural hematoma and it would be operated on the following morning.

The operation lasted about two hours. When the doctor came out, he informed the three that it was a complete success and Charlotte was in recovery. "When will we be able to see her?" asked Eloise. "Give her time to recover from the anesthetic. Why don't you go have lunch, and by then she will be ready to receive you."

After lunch, they returned to the hospital and were directed to Charlotte's room. Sitting up in bed with her head wrapped in bandages, Charlotte greeted them with a big smile. "Although it hurts a bit, I feel better than I have since I took that tumble." Everyone clapped and congratulated the patient. Four days after, Charlotte returned home.

Chapter 63

Life settled into a normal routine. Charlotte was back to her old self, even with a bit more energy than before. They went to the theater and dined out often. Eloise outgrew her clothes and was compelled to purchase larger and larger items for her wardrobe. As the time of her delivery neared, Eloise was so big she had difficulty getting around. Concerned, Thomas asked the doctor if there was a problem. The doctor mischievously smiled, "Your wife is not carrying a child."

"What can you possibly mean?" asked Thomas. "Your missus is carrying not one but two. You are going to be a father of twins." Thomas was speechless but overjoyed. Twins had never even been mentioned.

When told of the twins Eloise exclaimed, "I wondered how two little feet could kick so much." Everyone laughed.

The following week, Eloise went into labor. The doctor was summoned and he attended to her. The birthing went quickly for a first-time mother and resulted in a boy and a girl. "Now it's your turn," Sarah said laughingly. "I've already raised a baby."

Eloise looked at Thomas. "We must name our children for the birth certificates." Thomas responded, "I offer a deal. I'll name our son and you name our daughter."

"Agreed," answered Eloise. "Very well, our son shall be called Connor Elrod Rooney," Thomas replied.

"A fine, strong name," said Eloise, and Thomas told her, "Your turn, my love."

"Our daughter shall be named Muriel Ann Rooney." Sarah interjected, "Excellent Irish names." Charlotte teared up, knowing her grandson was named after her late husband. "Thank you, Thomas. Elrod would be very proud."

Chapter 64

Months went by and the children grew, and their grandmother and their aunt doted on them. Any talk of a nanny was met with questions: "Are we not doing well? Do you think a stranger would be better for our babies?"

"No, no that is not the reason. Grandmother is getting up in years and it is difficult for her to pick up the children. Sarah, you need to think about a family of your own, for you will make a wonderful mother." Sarah blushed. "I have been seeing a fellow," she said. "I thought so," said Charlotte. "I've noticed you being in a daze when you return from shopping, humming and singing to yourself."

"Faith and begorrah, that is welcomed news," exclaimed Thomas. "Who is this chap who has caught your fancy?"

"Just a nice fellow I see occasionally when I'm out shopping."

"Uh-huh, and when do we get to meet this fine fellow?"

"Let's not rush the lass, Thomas. These things take time," cautioned Charlotte.

"Now to the twins," said Sarah. "Do you really intend to employ a nanny?"

"We must," answered Eloise. For the better part of a year now, we have been attending business college. Now there are business matters that require our attention in Scotland and back in Ireland. Our distillery in Scotland is expanding and we must order larger copper stills. Before ordering we must be sure the building is capable of handling the new stills. If not, we will contract laborers to enlarge the structure."

"When will you be leaving?" asked Sarah.

"As soon as we locate a suitable nanny," Eloise told her.

The search for a nanny extended to newspaper ads and inquiries at the employment office. Several young ladies and a couple of not so young ladies were interviewed without success. Most did not want to handle two small children at the same time.

One afternoon a knock at the door was heard. Sarah opened the door to find a girl of about eighteen or nineteen standing on the stoop. The girl was very thin and appeared to be quite poor. Her clothes were little more than rags and she wore no shoes. On her head were the remnants of a scarf. The girl looked down at her feet when Sarah asked what she wanted. 'Please Ma'am, I heerd you was wanting to find a nanny."

"And you believe we should consider you for the position?"

"Yes Ma'am."

"Have you any experience taking care of children?"

"Oh yes. I am the oldest of eight children and did most of the tending to my brothers and sisters."

"Where is your family?"

"They are back in Ireland where they work on the farms."

"Why did you leave?"

"My da was going to sell me to an auld bugger for a wife."

"How did you come to be in Liverpool?"

"I sneaked onto the ferry at night and hid until it got here. I was fearful if I remained in Ireland, my father would seek me out."

"Step inside, I want the children's parents to meet you."

Thomas and Eloise were presented to the girl. The girl bobbed a curtsy then stood with her eyes downcast. Thomas and Eloise looked at Sarah with pleading eyes. Sarah spoke, "This cailin is interested in being your nanny."

"What have you in mind, dear sister?" asked Thomas. "Give me a few minutes to get your answer," she replied.

Sarah took the girl to the bathroom and instructed her to wash up. After the girl had cleaned her hands and arms, Sarah took her to the nursery where Thomas and Eloise waited. When the girl saw the twins, her face broke into a big smile. Sarah said, "Change their nappies." Immediately the girl removed the diaper, first from one then the other. Checking to see if they needed cleaning, she powdered each one and put on clean diapers. As she worked, she whispered to the babies and they seemed to be entranced by her. Sarah questioned the girl about bathing infants, feeding and clothing. She was asked how to tell if a child was distressed or uncomfortable, how to check for a fever and what to do when a child is teething. To each and every question she answered immediately and correctly.

"Seems we have us a nanny, Thomas," said Eloise.

They took the girl to meet Charlotte. "What is your name child?"

"Talulla Rafferty, Ma'am."

"Well Talulla Rafferty, we must get you cleaned up and settled in before dinner."

Talulla had her first bath in a long while, and her hair had not been acquainted with a comb for even longer. Eloise gave her some clothes and told her, "These will have to do until we can get you some of your own." Talulla looked very presentable. "Tomorrow, we will purchase you some shoes." Talulla's bed would be in the nursery with the twins.

At dinner everyone watched Talulla. The poor child was trying to eat in a ladylike fashion, though it was obvious she was famished. She hardly put a forkful in her mouth before she was loading up her fork with another bite. When everyone else had finished, Talulla continued to eat. She looked up in mid-bite to see the others were done and slowly put down her fork. "It is okay Talulla, you have some catching up to do. Go ahead and finish your meal." Upon finishing, Talulla excused herself and went to attend to the twins. Soon she returned and began to clear the dishes from the table. "Talulla, you are a nanny, not a housemaid. Your responsibility is the children."

"I don't mind Ma'am. I's use to doing house chores."

"Already you are looking to take my job," laughed Sarah.

Chapter 65

The following week Thomas and Eloise hired a motor car and driver to carry them to their distillery in Scotland. They had been on the road for a short time when Eloise said, “You were quite right, Thomas. The automobile is a superior method of travel.”

It was a comfortable and leisurely two-day drive from Liverpool to Lochaber, Scotland. The weather was mild and the countryside was beautiful. The gentle swaying of the vehicle had an almost hypnotic effect. Thomas and Eloise arrived in good spirits and proceeded immediately to Corncockle Estate Lodge in Lochaber. Over dinner they met with the master distiller and manager of the distillery. He had been a long time, trusted employee of the Rooney’s. He explained the need for new stills and with blueprints of the facility showed how the new stills would fit if one section was enlarged. Thomas made some subtle changes to the plans and all agreed on the outcome. After dinner, Sean McCauley set on the table a bottle of 20-year-old single malt, non-chill filtered Scotch whisky. After sipping a dram, Thomas declared it the finest he had ever tasted.

Their business concluded, Thomas and Eloise returned to the lodge. It had been a profitable day with their mission accomplished.

Chapter 66

The following morning, they began their journey back to Liverpool. A day later they arrived back home to find Talulla decked out in new finery and a fine pair of shoes. "She is a wonderful nanny," they were told by Sarah. "The twins adore her."

"That is good, for we must depart for Ireland rather soon." After spending as much time as they were able with the twins, Thomas and Eloise packed for their journey back to Ireland.

Upon arrival they proceeded directly to the Shelbourne on St Temples Green. Once in their room they freshened up and went down to the restaurant for dinner. Thomas ordered his favorite oysters and salmon. Eloise chose the chicken and mash. After a most enjoyable meal, they walked around town. Returning to their hotel they found Alford P. Little waiting for them. "Thank you for journeying to Dublin to meet with us Ms. Little. What intelligence did you bring?" Thomas asked.

"As you instructed me, I looked into the family of Talulla Rafferty. This is a truly sad story, one which I will have difficulty relaying to you. The Rafferty clan lives on a cropland farm out of Kilkenny. The family consists of Finn Rafferty, his wife Fiona and their eight children. The family is very poor and barely survives. Finn spends most of his time drinking whiskey while his wife and children labor in the fields. Finn is a cruel bugger to his family and anyone else he comes in contact with. Quick to anger and strike out, Finn is well known to the local garda. The children do not appear to attend school, nor is the family known to attend religious services. The parish priest said he once tried to intervene and offer the family some assistance. For his troubles, he was knocked to the ground by Finn and told never to come around his family. The oldest child Talulla disappeared about a fortnight back and hasn't been seen or heard of since."

Ms. Little continued, "The second oldest is a lad named Rian, he is the age of seventeen years. Rian is a stout lad and does his best to protect his mother and his siblings from his da's wrath. Next in line is a cailin by the name of Roisin who is fifteen. She is a lovely and gentle lass who is a wee bit simple minded. She rarely speaks and usually only to her mum or Rian. Roisin is terrified of her da and hides from him whenever she is able. Now comes the wicked part. A week back, Roisin informed Rian that her da had caught her hiding in the cow shed and had touched her under her clothing. Infuriated, Rian beat his da with a club, almost killing him. Finn will recover but will be partially paralyzed. Seems his days of abusing others has come to an end."

"And what about Rian, was he arrested?"

"Actually, the garda thought he should have finished the job on his da. He has not been charged with any crime," said Ms. Little. "Now what will happen to the family?" asked Eloise. "They are going to relocate north to a dairy farm where Fiona has a sister."

"And what about Finn?" asked Thomas. "Fiona insists she will take care of Finn. In her marriage vows she promised to be a faithful wife. Now that Finn is debilitated, he is no longer a threat to anyone and she refuses to desert him. She remembers what a good man he was before he took to drinking whiskey."

"Well, I suppose we should inform Fiona that Talulla is well and employed as a nanny. Surely, she must be concerned about her eldest child," suggested Eloise. "I will take care of informing her," said Ms. Little.

"Would you care to join us for dinner, Ms. Little?" asked Thomas. "I would be delighted," she replied. "Excellent, then let us join up at the Old Mill Restaurant by the Ha'penny Bridge at seven this evening."

Off went Ms. Little to a court appointment. Once word had gotten out that Alford P. Little was the barrister for the Rooney family, she had many clients, so many in fact that she could pick and choose who she wanted to represent.

Chapter 67

Thomas and Eloise attended several business meetings on Charlotte's behalf. Concluding their obligations, they proceeded to the Richmond Surgical Hospital on North Brunswick Street. They met with the chief surgeon, Doctor Rachel Dunnagan, who was a renowned surgeon. They described the disfigurement of Sister Mary Margaret. Doctor Dunnagan told them, "If what you have told me is accurate, I believe it is possible to restore most of this woman's features. I cannot be one hundred percent positive without seeing the facial damage and conducting an examination, though I am confident we can improve her appearance. Facial reconstruction is becoming common these days with great success," she offered. They thanked the good doctor and departed.

Thomas and Eloise decided on the morrow they would travel to Kilkenny and see if Sister Mary Margaret would like to undergo the procedure to restore her scarred face. The following morning, they took the stage to Kilkenny. The stage made numerous stops along the way, causing the journey to consume most of the day.

Arriving in the late afternoon, they found a room above a pub. Being quite exhausted from the journey, Eloise lay down on the bed to rest. Thomas said, "I will find out the location of the Convent and have a pint or two. I will come and collect you for dinner."

Thomas took a short walk to enjoy the fresh air then returned to the pub. Asking the proprietor where they would find the Convent, he was given the directions. The Convent was only a short way from where they were, easily within walking distance. Thomas relaxed and enjoyed a pint of ale. The ale and the warm fire were so comforting, Thomas dozed off. The bartender shook Thomas and asked, "Would you be wanting another pint, sir?" Thomas asked what time it was and discovered he had slept for almost an hour. "I'd best go up and bring my wife down for dinner," he explained.

Thomas went up to their room to find Eloise awake and dressed for dinner. "Give me a minute to wash up, love," he said. A few minutes later they were sitting at a table waiting for their meal. The serving girl brought them both lamb stew.

"I'm quite anxious to see Sister Mary Margaret again, she is such a sweet soul," said Eloise. " I do not believe I would be here nor would me mother had it not been for her kindness," answered Thomas. Finishing their dinner, they retired for the evening.

Chapter 68

After a hardy breakfast of eggs, boxty and toast, they walked to the Convent. The bell was answered by a young nun, and after stating their intentions, Sister Mary Margaret was summoned. "Has your residency here been an improvement over the last Convent?" Thomas asked. "Oh yes. The Sisters here are loving and kind. However, my family does not desire to visit me. They said it has been a long time since I went away, and I would only bring back sad memories."

"We are so sorry dear Sister," said Eloise. "Now we wish tell you of some intelligence we learned while in Dublin. Then Thomas told her of the meeting with Doctor Dunnagan and their offer to finance her medical care. Sister Mary Margaret began to weep. "What is the matter?" asked Thomas. Sister Mary Margaret answered, "What if God want's me this way?"

"You were but a wee child when the accident occurred. I cannot believe God intended you to go through life disfigured," said Eloise softly. "God gave the doctors the ability and knowledge to help people such as you, so it must be God's will that your disfigurement be corrected."

"I must pray before making a decision," stated Sister Mary Margaret. "Please allow me a few days to meditate."

"Certainly," replied Thomas. "There is no great hurry."

Thomas and Eloise left the Convent, vowing to return in one week to see if Sister Mary Margaret had arrived at a decision.

So for the next several days, Thomas and Eloise attended to business matters for Charlotte. After seven days had passed, they proceeded to the Convent with high hopes. After they were admitted to the Convent, Sister Mary Margaret appeared. She looked relaxed and happy. "Have you come to a decision, dear Sister?" Eloise asked.

"I have," the Sister replied. "First, I must enlighten you as to what I believe to be a miracle. After you left last week, I informed the Mother Superior of my dilemma. The Mother gathered all of the nuns together and asked them to fast and pray individually on my behalf. For three days and nights the entire Convent fasted and prayed. Our regular assignments were put on hold. The Sisters either prayed in the chapel or in their rooms. After the third day, the Mother Superior gathered us together and asked each nun what had resulted from their prayers. One by one, the nuns began to tell of their experience. Each one used almost the exact same words: 'The Lord wants his faithful servant healed.' Now I know I should have the surgery."

Thomas and Eloise were delighted. They hugged Sister Mary Margaret and wept with her. Thomas said, "I will schedule an appointment with Doctor Dunnagan. We will inform you when the time comes and will send a carriage to transport you and have a room at the hospital waiting."

Chapter 69

About a month went by to when the appointment was scheduled and Sister Mary Margaret traveled to Dublin. After many days of testing and preparing for the surgery, the event took place. Doctor Dunnagan and another doctor assistant, plus eight nurses applied their skill to the patient's face. The surgery took nine hours. Sister Mary Margaret went first to recovery then to her private room. Her whole head was wrapped in bandages. The doctor approached her and held her hand. "The surgery went better than expected," she told her. "I believe you will be most pleased with the results."

"How long before I can see myself?" she asked. "At least another week," the doctor replied. "We must take every precaution to prevent infection. The swelling and bruising will last for several days. Sometime a follow up surgery is necessary, though we are hopeful that's not in your case."

"Thank you doctor, I am quite tired."

"Rest now. I will check on you from time to time."

The healing process was slow and painful. Her only nourishment was in liquid form. There were times when Sister Mary Margaret wondered if it had been worth it.

Ten days after the surgery, Doctor Dunnagan took off the bandages and removed the stiches. "May I look?" asked Sister Mary Margaret. "Not yet," the doctor answered. "There is too much discoloration and swelling for you to observe at this point. The healing is slow and it looks far worse than it actually is. Seeing your face before it is healed would be discouraging to you."

Two weeks passed, when the doctor entered the room and said, "Today we remove the bandages for good." Slowly, the bandages were taken off and her new face was revealed. The doctor smiled. "The results exceeded my expectations," she said. "There remains some light bruising but the swelling has gone down."

A mirror was offered to Sister Mary Margaret. She slowly raised the mirror to where she could observe her face. "Is that me? Is that me?" she shouted. "I have a nose and lips. Look at my eye, it barely droops. I look normal! Oh, doctor how can I ever thank you?"

"Seeing your happiness is thanks enough," the good doctor replied. "I am so pleased I was able to help you."

Later that afternoon, Thomas and Eloise arrived at the hospital. After being ushered into the room where Sister Mary Margaret lay sleeping, Eloise whispered, "Dear, we have come to visit you." Sister Mary Margaret slowly turned and sat up. Thomas and Eloise started clapping and smiling. "You look wonderful. How do you feel?"

"I am so happy," she replied. "I cannot thank you enough for arranging this for me."

"We were happy to do it. I shall forever remember what you did for my mother and myself. It is you to be thanked," Thomas told her.

"Doctor Dunnagan said you would be discharged from the hospital soon. We have arranged transportation for you back to Kilkenny. We will visit whenever possible."

Some months later, Sister Mary Margaret had some errands in Kilkenny. As she was walking along, she observed a couple walking towards her. As the distance narrowed, she recognized her mother and father. As they passed, her father tipped his hat and said, "Good morning, Sister." Sister Mary Margaret nodded and kept walking. Under her breath she whispered, "Good morning, Da."

Chapter 70

Thomas and Eloise walked up to the O' Donnell house and knocked. Erin answered the door, and when she saw who the visitors were, she hugged and kissed Thomas, then Eloise. "I am so happy to see you both. Please come in."

Sitting at the kitchen table having tea was Duff and his wife. "You look quite robust, Grandfather," said Thomas. "Aye, I'm being cared for by two women who won't give me time to breath."

"You enjoy every minute of it Father," answered Erin. Everyone laughed. "How long will your visit be?" asked Erin. "Perhaps a couple of days.

No more, as we are scheduled to return to Liverpool in a fortnight." For the following two days everyone enjoyed being together. The women went shopping, while Thomas and Duff solved all of the world's problems over pints of Guinness.

As they departed Galway the next morning, Eloise turned to Thomas. "Do we have time to visit Mother this trip?"

"I believe we can spare a day or two," he answered.

Another journey of two days brought them to Kanturk. Joyce was hanging laundry on the line as they drove up. Eloise ran to her mother and they hugged and kissed. Thomas asked, "Is Loser about?"

"He is in school," she replied. "And how is that going?" he responded. "Well, after a shaky beginning, things are going rather well. Loser got into a couple of scraps over his name, though once the other lads realized he was a formidable foe, they stopped their teasing. Loser is extremely bright and an excellent student. Although he will not admit it, he enjoys school, and especially likes being around the lovely girls."

"Ah yes. He is about the age when young fellows become interested in the young ladies," Thomas laughed.

Chapter 71

Loser came home from school to a surprise. Not only were Thomas and Eloise there, but the celebration they never had a chance to enjoy was laid out on the table. Boiled beef, sausages, lamb stew, cabbage, carrots and plenty of ale. Thomas had hired some lads from the village to play music. One had a violin, one had a bodhran and the other had a guitar. They played and sang while everyone enjoyed the feast.

For two days they listened to Loser tell of his experiences and Joyce talked of reuniting with old friends and neighbors. Finally, Thomas informed everyone that they would be leaving in the morning. Loser asked if he had been adopted. "Not quite yet," Eloise told him. "The legal process is ongoing. There are some questions about your parents that are unanswered. Ms. Little is trying to sort it out and expects to have more information soon. As soon as the legalities are satisfied, the adoption petition will be presented to the court. In the meantime, continue your studies and watch over Joyce."

Thomas and Eloise departed the following morning. "Must we endure another ferry ride?" she asked. "I'm afraid so," Thomas answered. "This time the weather is supposed to be totally different." After arriving in Dublin, they proceeded to the home of Mary McGuire. Ms. McGuire was beside herself with joy over seeing her former boarders. "Come in, come in, dear friends. How good it is to see you again."

"Have you a room for us, Mary?"

"I do, of course I do," she said cheerily. "How long will you be staying?" she asked. "Just tonight. We leave on the morning ferry." Mary insisted on preparing her lamb stew for them. "You will find no argument from us," Thomas laughed. After dinner and a time spent telling of their experiences, the couple retired.

Chapter 72

The next morning, bright and early they proceeded to the docks and boarded the ferry. The weather was clear, the sun shining and the water was calm as far as the eye could see. This time, the trip was uneventful. After debarking in Liverpool, they hired a buggy and went directly home. First stop was the nursery to hug and kiss the twins. "My goodness Thomas. Look how they have grown," said Eloise excitedly.

Talulla had been an excellent nanny and the twins were clean and healthy. Next, Thomas and Eloise met with Charlotte and Sarah. They explained the circumstances with Talulla's family, and elaborated on the surgery performed on Sister Mary Margaret. Charlotte was pleased with the business end of their trip and congratulated them both. Charlotte glanced over at Sarah and said, "We have some news for you as well."

"What is it?" asked Eloise.

"It seems our Sarah has a serious beau."

"Sarah, tell us all about it," pleaded Eloise. Blushing, Sarah said, "My friend you knew about before you left has become quite dear to me. We see each other almost every time I am in town. Charlotte has permitted Richard to accompany me home from town and with your acceptance, I may invite him to dinner."

"Richard, is it?" said Thomas.

"Yes, Richard Chapman is his name."

"And what does Richard Chapman do, Sarah?"

"Actually, it is Sir Richard," Sarah said. "Richard was knighted for his service in the Royal Navy. His family owns a horse breeding farm and Richard runs it."

"How did you actually meet?" asked Thomas.

"A rather lengthy story it is," said Sarah. "It began many months ago. Richard was in town on business when he noticed me at the market. He had asked one of the merchants about me, but all they knew was that I shopped every Monday. After that Richard made it a point to be at the market every Monday. After several weeks, he decided he must meet me. Knowing I usually shopped with Charlotte, and she is well known in town, he inquired about me through common acquaintances. Sir Richard sent a note to Charlotte asking if he could call on me. Charlotte informed him that his request was being considered. Of course, I did not know any of this until after we had become friends."

Thomas turned to Charlotte, "Now we're a match maker, are we?"

"I've known about Richard's family for quite some time. His family has had accounts with the bank Elrod was president of. Sir Richard has always been a confirmed bachelor. Numerous young ladies have worked their wiles on him to no avail. He usually has a beautiful lady from one of the aristocratic families on his arm. With a reputation as a rogue and womanizer, I had many concerns about his attraction to our Sarah," Charlotte informed them.

"Like Elrod, I know many people in important positions. I had my solicitor hire an investigator to look into this chap's life. Although his reputation is not pristine, he has never had a hint of scandal where women are concerned, and he is certainly not a womanizer, showing nothing but total respect for women of all ages. Even those ladies who tried and failed to win him over had nothing but the highest regards and respect for him."

Charlotte continued, "After that report, I arranged a meeting with Sir Richard. In this meeting, he assured me that his intentions regarding Sarah were honorable. He related that he was immediately attracted to her not just because of her beauty, but to the way in which she carried herself with poise and dignity. He admired how she interacted with others and the kindness she showed toward everyone, especially those less fortunate. She appeared to him as special before he even knew her. After watching her for some time he sent me the note. Sir Richard checked out to my complete satisfaction."

"Well, that suits me. I wouldn't want my sister to keep company with just any Tom, Dick or Harry," said Thomas, to which everyone had a good laugh.

"With your permission Thomas, I would like to invite Sir Richard to dinner and permit him to call on Sarah," said Charlotte. "And your thoughts, dear sister?" asked Thomas. Sarah blushed, "I would like to have Sir Richard call on me."

"Then it is settled. We shall invite Sir Richard to dine with us next Saturday. I will dispatch an invitation this very afternoon," said Charlotte. True to her word, Charlotte sent the invitation by messenger immediately after tea.

Chapter 73

In preparation for the upcoming dinner, Charlotte, Sarah and Eloise attacked the interior of the house. When they were done after two days, not a speck of dust could be found, nor a smudge on a window. While the ladies toiled inside, Thomas with equal enthusiasm did likewise to the yard. Every leaf was raked, every bush was trimmed. Their collective efforts resulted in the home being as cared for as it had ever been.

Next item was the dinner itself. Charlotte was to prepare roast beef and pheasant. Sarah was to contribute the potatoes, gravy, salad and Yorkshire pudding. Eloise was in charge of dessert, and chose strawberry fool. Thomas' contribution was the dinner wine and the after-dinner brandy.

Charlotte engaged the service of a woman to help in the kitchen and a manservant to serve food and drink. Talulla was to present the twins in their finest apparel and fully fed before the adults dined. She would retire with them once the dinner was served. She was also charged with keeping the children under control while the guest was present.

Saturday arrived with great expectation. The ladies were all in a tizzy getting their hair just perfect and deciding which dress to wear. Sarah was especially panicked. She would try on a dress, ask everyone's opinion then try on another and ask the same thing. After four dresses, the ladies got together and convinced Sarah that the first one was absolutely the best. It did not end there, and different hair styles became a concern. As with the dresses, Sarah presented herself with different coiffures. As the ladies debated over the various hairstyles, Thomas found it so amusing that he burst out laughing. Sarah, believing he was laughing at her present hair presentation began to weep.

Eloise gave Thomas a look that ceased his jocularity instantly.

Taking the not-so-subtle hint, Thomas took himself to the nursery and occupied himself playing with the twins. With Thomas caring for the twins, Talulla asked, "Sir might I be excused so I may join the ladies?"

"Certainly," replied Thomas. "But a word of advice, do not laugh."

Nearing the time for dinner, the door knocker sounded. Thomas answered the door and welcomed their guest, Sir Richard. "I have been looking forward to meeting you since I was informed of your interest in my sister," he said. Sir Richard and Thomas shook hands. Sir Richard was in possession of a very large bouquet of flowers and a rather large box of candy. The guest was ushered into the drawing room and there introduced to the ladies. Sir Richard gave the box of candy to Charlotte and bowing kissed her hand. Next he bowed to Sarah and handed her the flowers. Sarah gave a slight curtsey as she accepted the gift. Sir Richard bowed to Eloise and kissed her hand. "An honor to meet you, Madam."

With the formalities completed, everyone retired to the dining room. The meal was as delicious as it was attractive. Throughout the meal, Sir Richard was rather quiet, as was Sarah. Thomas and Charlotte made efforts to keep a friendly banter going over an otherwise subdued meal. After completion of their dinner, all retired to the drawing room for brandy.

Somewhat more relaxed, everyone joined in the conversation. Sir Richard told of his experiences in the Navy and of his love for horses. Thomas and Eloise told of some of their experiences in Ireland. Sir Richard did not appear to have any animosity toward the Irish. In fact, he was sympathetic to many of their grievances. The evening concluded on a most pleasant note with promises of getting together again soon. Sir Richard asked if he might take Sarah to his horse farm the following Friday, as there was to be a sale of yearlings and mares.

Thomas asked Sir Richard, "Will you be chaperoned?" Sir Richard looked confused. Charlotte laughed until tears ran down her cheeks. Sarah spoke, "Thomas dear, both Sir Richard and myself are at an age where a chaperone is not necessary and I assure you, unwanted. I accept the invitation and look forward to seeing your horse farm," Sarah directed to Sir Richard.

Chapter 74

For many months thereafter, Charlotte, Thomas and Eloise attended to the family businesses. Talulla attended to the twins, who were now learning to talk. Their parents were both loving, attentive and involved in every phase of their children's lives.

The relationship between Sarah and Sir Richard blossomed into love. They were a lovely couple and everyone anticipated the announcement of a wedding in the near future. Throughout the upper-class social society, it was a different story. Once it was learned that Sarah was a commoner, she was vilified. Aristocracy could not accept such a union. Newspaper articles referred to Sarah as a gold digger who didn't know her place. Rejected ladies called her vulgar and crass.

This attitude negatively affected Sarah, and she suggested to Sir Richard that she was beneath him and perhaps they should reconsider their relationship. At this suggestion Sir Richard was enraged. "That does it," he proclaimed. "Dropping to one knee, he held Sarah's hands in his and asked, "Sarah I will love you forever and a day. Will you honor me by becoming my wife?" Sarah began to weep tears of joy. "Are you quite sure, dear Richard?"

"As sure as I have ever been in my life," he answered.

"My greatest joy will be as your wife."

Sir Richard stood and embraced Sarah. "I will ask my mother to begin preparations for our wedding. It will be the social event of the year. Those few who maligned you are not to be invited. That should set them straight." Richard further offered, "Tomorrow we shall go shopping for an engagement ring."

"I do not require anything fancy or ostentatious, my love," said Sarah. "We shall have one designed especially for you, Sarah."

"Oh Richard, a simple ring will be quite enough," she replied. "I think not my love. You are an uncommon creature and the personification of grace and beauty. You must have a ring that matches those unique qualities."

Sarah could hardly wait until she could inform everyone that she was engaged.

Chapter 75

Upon returning home later that afternoon, Sarah asked everyone to assemble in the drawing room. Once all were seated, Sarah began asking one then another about their day and did they have plans for the weekend. "Come, come," invoked Thomas, "you did not invite us here to ask about our day. What are your true intentions for this meeting?"

Sarah blushed and began to speak. "Today Sir Richard asked me to be his wife and I accepted." Immediately all assembled began laughing, clapping and shouting congratulations. All took turns hugging and kissing Sarah. Then the questions began. "When will the wedding take place?" asked Eloise. "Where will the event be held?" asked Charlotte. "Will I be permitted to attend?" asked Talulla. "Please, please one question at a time," laughed Sarah.

"First Talulla, of course you will be invited and I pray you will consider being one of my bridesmaids." Talulla began to weep. "Oh yes, it will be such an honor for me."

"Good, then that is settled," replied Sarah.

"Next question. We have not yet begun the planning. As far as when or where, I am unsure of at the present time. I will enlighten you as soon as the arrangements have been sorted out."

Sir Richard did the same as Sarah, and asked his family to assemble as he had an announcement to make. Informing his parents and siblings of his engagement, he was confronted with blank stares. His father spoke, "Son have you fully considered the ramifications of you marrying a commoner?"

"What ramifications can there be? Once she and I are married she will no longer be a commoner?"

"She will always be a commoner in the eyes of our friends and associates," his mother added. "I will be the laughing stock of my girl friends," his sister said while she blew her nose. "If our so-called friends do not accept my decision, then they are no longer my friends," Sir Richard responded.

"Does that include family?" asked his brother. "Are you saying my own family would be against my marrying the love of my life?" Richard said angrily. "It will just take some time for us to understand your choice," said his father.

"It seems you are more concerned about how people will accept my marriage than you are about my choice and my happiness." No one spoke. Richard stood up and looked at each of his family members. He shook his head and began walking away. His mother called, "Richard, I have saved your great grandmother's ring for your bride. However, I cannot in good faith allow it to be given to this girl."

"Her name is Sarah and she is not a girl. She is a beautiful and intelligent woman and I am blessed to even know her. Do not concern yourself regarding a ring Mother, Sarah and I have an appointment with the jewelers tomorrow and will be having a ring created for her." His mother gasped.

Richard turned and walked out of the room. As he went down the hall, his name was called. "Richard, wait up." He turned and saw his youngest brother coming. Richard stopped, expecting further chastisement. His sixteen-year-old brother Malcolm stuck out his hand. "Shake brother and congratulations. I'm looking forward to meeting your Sarah. That was great watching you defend yourself and Sarah. Who gives a damn about a bunch of old stuffed shirts anyway?" Richard broke into laughter. "Thanks little brother. I appreciate your support."

Chapter 76

In the ensuing months, a ring was purchased, a wedding dress was sewn, the church was reserved for the wedding, participants were selected, the after- ceremony feast was ordered, and the very short guest list was composed. The guest list included very few of Sir Richard's acquaintances, only a few who had never voiced any negativism toward the union. Conspicuously absent was most of Sir Richard's family. Only Malcolm's name graced the list.

A month prior to the wedding date, Charlotte decided to throw a bridal shower, usually a gift-giving party held for the bride-to-be in anticipation of her wedding. But Charlotte did not have her thoughts on the usual intentions of such an event. Her desire was to heal the rift in Richard's family, the Chapmans. Charlotte hired Becky Richards, a caterer she knew who was often used by the Chapmans to throw lavish parties. Her knowledge of the Chapman's preferences for food and drink helped Charlotte decide on the menu.

The guest list included Sir Richard's immediate family and many of his social acquaintances. Praying for success, Charlotte had the RSVP invitations delivered by messenger.

It was but two days prior to the bridal shower, and although there were many RSVPs, none were from the Chapman family. Charlotte was dispirited, though not altogether surprised.

The afternoon of the shower, Thomas and Sir Richard made themselves scarce by heading to Ye Hole in Ye Wall, the oldest pub in Liverpool.

Chapter 77

The bridal shower began slowly, as many of those in attendance were there merely to see the commoner Sarah. Charlotte began to believe the idea was not a very good one. Sarah being the gracious and gentle person that she was, began to soften hearts. Once meeting her, guests could find no fault or reason not to admire and respect her.

About an hour after the shower began, the door knocker announced the presence of someone on the stoop. Charlotte opened the door to discover Sir Richard's mother and his sisters. Although in a bit of shock, Charlotte greeted her guests and invited them in. After taking their coat, she ushered the ladies into the room where the shower was being held.

All looked at the arrivals and silence prevailed. Sarah slowly walked over to Mrs. Chapman. She curtsied, kissed the lady's hand and said, "I am so sorry I have caused you distress, dear Mother. Please forgive me." Mrs. Chapman was silent for a moment. Then with tears in her eyes, she stepped forward and embraced Sarah. "I came here to see for myself what kind of person you are. It is I who need to ask for forgiveness. I can understand why my son fell in love with you. I am pleased to welcome you into our family." The whole room resounded with applause and laughter. Then the real party began.

Thomas and Sir Richard mulled over what was transpiring back at the house. "I just hope the house is still standing," voiced Thomas.

Upon returning home, Thomas and Sir Richard entered the house rather slowly. It appeared the guests had departed, for the house was rather quiet. Then they heard activity in the drawing room and headed there. Upon entering, they immediately looked at each other, for there on the sofa was Richard's mother enjoying a glass of brandy. His sisters were also present, sipping wine. Sir Richard looked at Sarah, who smiled and said, "I have met your wonderful mother my dear and your beautiful sisters." Thus ended the bridal shower where the most treasured gift came from the heart of Charlotte.

The wedding took place as scheduled. With Sir Richard's family now supporting the union, the entire celebration grew exponentially. Becky Richards was engaged to cater the reception, saying it was the most elaborate reception she had ever done.

With the twins needing less and less attention from their nanny, Talulla was promoted to Sarah's old position in addition to her child care responsibilities.

Charlotte was enjoying her final years with a real family. She doted on the twins and constantly lavished them with gifts.

Thomas and Eloise made many trips to Ireland, taking the twins to meet and spend time with their grandmothers. They also traveled to Australia and New Zealand, and the businesses flourished under their watchful eyes and sound business decisions.

Chapter 78

One afternoon, Charlotte, Thomas and Eloise were musing over their lives. "We have done well and accomplished just about everything we set out to do," Charlotte offered.

"There is one thing I must still do," said Thomas.

"What is that, my dear?" inquired Eloise.

"I must confront the scoundrel who fathered me and condemned my mother to the Magdalene Laundry."

Irish Dictionary

Auld	Old
Bangers and mash	Sausage and mashed potatoes
Barrister/Solicitor	Lawyers
Bodhran	Irish drum
Boxty	Mashed and shredded potato patties
Black and White Pudding	Sausage patties black with pig blood
Bullocks	An insult
Cailin	Girl
Cove	Boy street child
Da	Father
Eejit	Idiot
Faith and Begorra	By golly or by gosh
Garda/Garda Siochana	Police
Maimeo	Grandmother
Mo Anam Cara	My soul mate
Mum	Mother
Paddy `	A brand of Irish whiskey
Pinched	Arrested
Portmanteau	A suitcase
Potin/poteen/potcheen	Irish moonshine
Shirred eggs	Egg, butter and cream baked in a dish
Strawberry Fool	Strawberries and cream
Tosser	Obnoxious jerk
Wanker	One who masturbates

About the Author

John Hodge was eighty-four years old when this book was published. The intent of this book was to leave his children and grandchildren a remembrance of his story telling. He was the middle of three children born to John and Gertrude Hodge, with an older sister Joyce and younger brother Richard.

John graduated high school in 1956 and immediately began working as a firefighter for the California Division of Forestry. After the fire season he was employed at the Napa State Hospital as a Psychiatric Technician in training.

A year later John joined the U.S. Navy. After completing training, he was stationed on the USS Mills DER 383 out of Newport, Rhode Island.

In 1959 John married his girlfriend, Darlene Hayes. John and Darlene had three children, Connie, Dawn and Stephen.

Honorably discharged from the Navy in 1963, John was hired by the Eastman Kodak Company as a service technician for microfilm equipment. Fourteen years later John left Kodak to operate a drive-in restaurant staffed by his wife and children.

John held several managerial positions before becoming a counselor at the Missoula Pre-Release Center. After attending the Law Enforcement Academy, John was a Probation and Parole Officer for the Montana Department of Corrections until he retired in 2003.

John and Darlene divorced in 1999. In 2005 John married his current wife Thoralee Dean. Thoralee has two children, Kimberly and Kari. Between them, John and Thoralee have thirteen grandchildren and fourteen great-grandchildren.

John and Thoralee currently reside in Somers, Montana with their Mini-Aussie, Lucy.

I never lie, I do however have my own version of the truth.

John Hodge

Made in United States
North Haven, CT
19 June 2025